Ten Twists

To Donna,
Enjoy the stories.
—Geaux Saints
R. Guero
11/11/11

Ten Twists

Ruben Quero

AuthorHouse™
1663 Liberty Drive
Bloomington, IN 47403
www.authorhouse.com
Phone: 1-800-839-8640

© *2011 by Ruben Quero. All rights reserved.*

No part of this book may be reproduced, stored in a retrieval system, or transmitted by any means without the written permission of the author.

First published by AuthorHouse   10/17/2011

ISBN: 978-1-4670-2832-5 (sc)
ISBN: 978-1-4670-2833-2 (hc)
ISBN: 978-1-4670-2831-8 (ebk)

Library of Congress Control Number: 2011915907

Printed in the United States of America

Any people depicted in stock imagery provided by Thinkstock are models, and such images are being used for illustrative purposes only.
Certain stock imagery © Thinkstock.

This book is printed on acid-free paper.

Because of the dynamic nature of the Internet, any web addresses or links contained in this book may have changed since publication and may no longer be valid. The views expressed in this work are solely those of the author and do not necessarily reflect the views of the publisher, and the publisher hereby disclaims any responsibility for them.

The stories in this book may contain some true events and locations, however, used in a fictitious setting. All characters, businesses, and dialogues are products of the author's imagination and are not to be construed as real. Any resemblance to persons, living or dead, is entirely coincidental.

This book is dedicated to my siblings:

Yoli, Rita, Vicky, Ginny, France, Larry,
and
to my partner Jerry

In memory of my parents:

Cirelo M. Quero
(1906-1990)

Mary Helen Barajas Quero
(1928-2009)

The leafs within this binding are few,
there are only ten twists for you
to pick up and read, a story that's short,
as you sip and enjoy your port.

If your choice of beverage is tea,
and often you're required to pee,
just put the book down, as your bladder insists,
and later . . . come back for the twist.

—R. Quero

TABLE OF TWISTS

Angelika 3
Family Photos 19
Hobo Jungle 33
Little Lady 47
Katie 55
Born to Dance 67
In A World of Silence 75
The Cruise 81
The Life of Lu Wang 95
A Short Love Story 117
Note to the Reader 127
Acknowledgements 129
About the Author 131

ANGELIKA

*Through the eyes of the world she was,
a woman that heads she could cause,
to turn and to gawk, as she strutted her stuff,
in front of them, they wished she would pause.*

*She now finds herself on a farm,
protecting her pets from all harm.
On guard with a rifle, and a cup of hot tea,
not knowing what her target might be.*

—R. Quero

Angelika

The tall lanky woman sat on her front porch enduring the unusually cool, brisk temperature brought on by the arrival of early fall weather. It was nine-thirty at night and she sat perfectly still. Her eyes fixed on the edge of the wooded area that butted up to her property line. On her lap she delicately cradled her grandfather's favorite 30/30 rifle.

Spanning a period of six nights straight, her henhouse had been raided and, to make matters worse, two of her prize miniature goats were taken from their pen. A thick layer of pine straw precluded any form of imprint from being left behind. Blood on the ground, however, was evidence that the killings were committed within the well-constructed animal shelters. Other than the latched gates, the only way in was to fly into or to scale the six foot chain link fence.

Only once, did Annie or Naomi, her live-in nurse, hear anything. By the time they made it downstairs, whatever was taking her animals had hurriedly vanished into the darkness of the night. "We'll catch that critter tonight," Annie vowed.

Annie sat there determined to wait out the culprit. The night air was making her drowsy, or maybe it was the hot tea Naomi prepared for her.

Naomi, concerned for her patient's health, placed a blanket over Annie's shoulders and wrapped it around and over her lap.

"You're gonna catch a nasty cold sitting out here all night long. I wish you would come inside," Naomi pleaded, gently patting her on the back with her large bronze hand.

"I'll be all right Naomi. You know I have to stay out here till I catch the thief that's been raiding the henhouse and stealing my goats. Patience is my strategy. I can easily outlast the hunger of that predator. I have a feeling that tonight I'll catch that culprit."

It was virtually pitch black with the exception of those brief moments when the moon managed to show its face through the layer of dark, grayish cumulus clouds. A light gentle breeze intermittently broke the stillness of the night, rustling the leaves that yet remained on the strong, majestic oak trees. The tall southern pines gracefully swayed to the change in air currents.

"What a wonderful, peaceful night," Annie thought out loud. "It brings back memories of when I was nine years old. My grandparents took me to the Caribbean on vacation. The tropical trade winds gently moved the palm trees and I thought they were waving at me." She took a slow, long sip of hot tea from her large, insulated mug.

The crunch from dried leaves being stepped on caught their attention. They both squinted as they focused in the direction of the noise. A few seconds seemed like eternity as the two scanned the dark woods. "Just a mama possum and her babies," whispered Naomi, with a sigh of relief.

"I never told you this Annie, but I'm glad you decided to keep the farm."

"Yeah, me too. It's been my home since childhood and has always been a place of solace and comfort for me. Even after the accident, just being here seems to help relieve some of these persistent and tormenting pains. I guess grandpa knew what he was doing when he willed the farm to me."

❑ ❑ ❑

Annie's mother died, due to uncontrollable hemorrhage, shortly after giving birth to her. Her father, a military man who suffered from post-traumatic stress disorder, was unable to cope with the death of his young wife. He tragically ended his own life, leaving his two month old daughter to be raised by her maternal grandparents.

"As you well know, they were the only family I knew," Annie spoke of her beloved grandparents with Naomi. "Without question or doubt, they raised me just like they did mother twenty years earlier. They raised me just like mom, a farm girl, on these thirty acres of lush rolling hills. They dedicated their lives to make sure I had a good one."

When Annie was eleven years old, her grandmother suffered a major stroke and Naomi, a home health nurse, was hired to care for the ailing senior. The damage from the massive cranial bleed was irreversible and after three months she passed away in her sleep.

"I remember that night," Naomi said, "your grandpa assumed the role of a single parent. Overnight he had to start learning how to provide the stability and encouragement that you as a young teenage girl needed."

"Actually, it was a team effort. Grandpa's health required semi-weekly home healthcare visits and he requested your services. You just happened to be there when I needed guidance and advice as I struggled through my teenage years and puberty. You were even there to help me work through the emotional hurt of breaking up with my first boyfriend. It was like having an older sister. We've always considered you part of the family. So after my accident the only person I wanted at my side caring for me was you, Naomi. I'm glad you were available and willing to take on the task."

◻ ◻ ◻

The four years Annie spent at college, along with her brief professional career were the only years she was away from the family farm. It was literally, her home-sweet-home and she had always dreamed of returning and retiring in the country when she reached those rocking chair years.

How ironic, Annie thought, *all I ever thought about was spending my retirement years on this porch and in this old rocking chair. Now, as fate would have it, here I am . . . home again.*

On any other night, at this hour she would normally be curled up in her soft, fluffy bed with an adventure or romance novel and sipping her tea.

A couple of cups of hot lemon tea, with a splash of bourbon, had become a nightly ritual. The tea, along with her regimen of prescribed pain killers, helped to calm and relax her.

Five long years, following the accident and ensuing surgeries, the pain still lingered. Even on her best days, she was in constant battle with excruciating pain. Not only was she hurting physically, but she also had the psychological trauma, which turned her life inside out, to contend with.

She took a sip of her hot tea and sat there, with Naomi at her side, patiently waiting. "You still awake?"

"Yep, little sister."

They both chuckled.

▫ ▫ ▫

It was the summer of 1996 and Annie had her suitcases all packed. She was ready to leave for college. A new life awaited her. Leaving grandpa proved to be one of the hardest things she'd ever done. She clutched the picture they had taken together at her high school graduation. *This picture,* she told herself, *I'll keep on my nightstand, so that every time I see it I'll be reminded of the wonderful times Grandpa and I had together.*

"Is it time to go Annie?" asked her Grandpa, starting to choke up.

Tears filled her beautiful green eyes. She hugged her grandfather and felt his body quiver, as she too fought back her own tears.

"This is for you," he said handing her a tiny box. "Go ahead and open it. It was your Grandma's pearl ring. I want you to have it."

"Thank you Grandpa. It's beautiful. I'll always treasure it. I love you so much."

Her grandfather and Naomi helped load the suitcases, books, and items needed in the dormitory. She climbed into her blue, two-seat convertible and started the ignition. She waved goodbye and drove off keeping an eye on her rear view mirror until they were no longer in sight.

▫ ▫ ▫

Annie started college bent on a career in fashion design. Ever since her childhood, she always enjoyed working with colors, patterns, and various textures. Creating different styles and matching them to a diverse group of people and their tastes appeared to be her forte.

"There isn't a better combination," she would tell her classmates, "than my two passions . . . people and fashion."

One day after class, Mr. Blackwell, one of Annie's professors asked to speak with her. "Annie, your designs are unique and you have an eye for details, but have you ever considered modeling? You're quite an attractive lady and I really believe you would do well as a model. Have you ever given that a thought?"

"I've always enjoyed the designing facet of the fashion industry, but I'd be lying if I said I never thought about what it would be like to model."

"Tell you what Annie," her professor said, "I had dinner with a colleague last night. He'll be introducing a new line of spring fashions at the Cherry Blossom Festival next month. He mentioned that he was considering using fresh, new talent to model some of his ladies' sportswear. Think you'd be interested?"

"Wow. I don't know, let me . . ." she started to reply.

"It'll be a short and fast show and will probably run no longer than thirty minutes max. Each model will only make one or two appearances," Mr. Blackwell said cutting her off. "He pays well and it'll give you that opportunity to get a feel for what it's like to actually model. What do you say, Annie?"

"Gosh, I've no experience in modeling. I'm afraid I might ruin the show and get completely laughed out of the industry."

"Annie, Mario DeMilano and his staff will coach you on what to do. You just need to get there a couple of hours before the show so they can size the garments and give you a chance to practice walking the runway."

"Mario DeMilano! Are you kidding me? Not 'the' Mario DeMilano?"

"That's right Annie. Listen, here's what I'll do. If you do the show I'll count it as your final project for my class. Do we have a deal? Can I call and tell him I found someone new?"

"All right Mr. Blackwell I'll give a try. If it doesn't work I can always chalk it up as experience."

"Great. To be quite honest, last night you're the first person that popped into my mind when I was talking with Mario. I have no doubt that you'll do just fine and I do believe you'll have fun modeling."

The show went on without any glitches. "I really enjoyed doing this," Annie told the other models. "I think I could get used to this line of work."

"Miss Summers," Mr. DeMilano called out to Annie, "you're a natural. I'd like to use you in other shows. I'd also be glad to circulate your name throughout the industry . . . that is if you want the extra work?"

During the next few months, Annie had offers to model hats, scarves, coats, dresses, and shoes. After graduation from college she spent more time modeling than designing.

Her big break came unexpectedly.

"Annie," Mr. DeMilano's secretary said on the phone, "five of our top models are stricken with the swine flu and Mr. DeMilano would like to have you show his line of clothes. The show is slated as one of New York City's biggest charity events and is sponsored by the world's top fashion designers. Can you help out?"

"I don't think I'm good enough for such an important show," Annie nervously confided.

"I've seen you walk the ramp and work the crowd, Annie. Mr. DeMilano has also seen you model. He wouldn't make you this offer if he didn't think you were capable. It's rare that he asks for a model by name. Annie, if I were young and beautiful as you are, I wouldn't pass this up. Trust me, you'll do OK."

▫ ▫ ▫

The night of the show Annie looked at the other girls and told them, "I'm a total wreck. I'm nothing but a bundle of nerves and you all look so calm."

"Annie, you'll do fine. Just go out there and be yourself," they told her as she prepared to debut at her first major, nationally televised, show for a world renowned designer.

Thinking that the name "Annie" was too blasé for a model, the flamboyant master of ceremonies introduced her to the audience, "Our next model is an angel in disguise. Wearing an elegant, black mid-calf evening gown, by designer Mario DeMilano, she is the beautiful and talented 'Angelika' . . . . that's Angelika with a 'K'."

The show was a huge success and Angelika, literally, became the talk of the town. That night she not only captured the hearts of the audience and the eyes of the designers, but she also caught the attention of the ever-so-cynical fashion critics.

Virtually overnight, Annie was catapulted from an unknown part-time model to one of America's leading models. Her tall slender built, her light brown hair, and her sensuous green eyes helped make Angelika a hot commodity in the commercial arena.

Some magazine articles described her as sensuous, while others labeled her an "American Angel". "She was born for the eye of the camera," they wrote. "She's a natural. Her facial expressions, body language, and candid poses outshine all other models on the runway of every show."

One fashion critic said of the young model, "Angelika is synonymous to gold . . . She is gold."

▫ ▫ ▫

Since then, five long, agonizing years had elapsed.

Now, here in the old rocking chair, staring into the night, her pain, again, triggered thoughts of the accident that stole her once prospering career and status as a supermodel . . . thoughts that repeatedly infiltrated her quiet moments and continued to whittle away at her peace of mind.

She resumed her silent gaze into the dark surroundings, reached out and took another sip from the insulated cup.

"It was on a night similar to this one," Annie broke a thirty minute silence, "when I received that call from you," she said glancing at Naomi. "You told me it would be a good idea to come and see Grandpa because he was now bedridden and required twenty-four hour care. I could tell by the tone in your voice that Grandpa was bad off."

"The last time I had seen him was six months earlier for his eighty-ninth birthday. The three of us had a wonderful time together."

"Your grandfather worshipped the ground you walked on," Naomi interjected. "I remember how proud he was to be seen with you, the 'number one-rated model' in the country. He beamed from ear-to-ear the entire time we were in that restaurant."

"I know Naomi, but even then he appeared slightly frail. He just wasn't the sprite, energetic man I knew all my life. It hurt to see that his health was rapidly deteriorating," Annie sadly recalled.

"But when I got that call I had a gut feeling that his time was at hand. I decided it would be a lot faster to drive rather than to fly and spend hours waiting on connecting flights. I reached you on the car phone and you held the phone so Grandpa could talk with me."

He told me, "Don't worry about me. I'm in excellent hands. Naomi is right here taking good care of me."

▫ ▫ ▫

Angelica exited the interstate about four miles from her childhood home. She was one mile from the private road that led up to the farm house and could feel the excitement mounting as the reunion with her ailing grandfather neared. *It sure will be great to see Gramps again,* she thought, as she got closer to the farm. *He looked so frail last time I was with him. Lord please let him gain his strength,* she silently prayed.

She never made it to his bedside. More than anything else, this she regretted.

Weeks later, she was finally able to share with Naomi, "I remember a truck passing me up. It was a white, flatbed truck hauling unsecured lumber. I hung up the phone after talking with Grandpa and made sure I was maintaining a safe distant between me and the other driver. The fog slowed us down. We were both traveling approximately fifty miles per hour. Although the fog was getting thicker by the minute, I still had a good view of that vehicle. Then for some unknown reason, the driver of the truck slammed on his brakes. The cargo slid off the bed of the truck, bounced off the pavement and headed directly toward my car. I swerved to avoid getting hit by the flying debris, but was still struck by ricocheting lumber and wooden posts."

The impact of the airborne logs instantly knocked Angelika unconscious. Her car, now driverless and out-of-control, careened off the road and slammed into a weeping willow. Ironically, it came to a standstill directly across the road from where the truck had stopped. The six to eight foot projectiles penetrated her car like pub missiles on a dartboard. One impacted the radiator and three went through the windshield. The safety air bags were slashed by the jagged planks of wood before they were fully deployed. Shattered glass, large splinters of lumber, and the crushing blow from the steering wheel all contributed to the horrific damage of Angelika's upper torso and the disfigurement to the right side of her face.

The accident investigation unit determined that after the truck lost its cargo, the driver pulled over to the side of the road. Skid marks indicated that the driver screeched away from the scene of the accident.

Another driver, who did not witness the accident first hand, confirmed their findings. He reported, "I saw a white truck that was stopped over there, hurriedly drive off."

The doctors were amazed, "Other than some internal bruises, none of your vital organs were seriously damaged. Your rib cage sustained the blunt of the force, leaving you with multiple broken and shattered ribs," they filled her in on her medical condition. "Shards of glass and large splinters of wood tore flesh and muscle off your lean body and badly lacerated the right side of your face."

"You know, you're pretty lucky things didn't turn out any worse," the anesthesiologist told her on the morning of one of her many reconstructive surgeries.

"Doctor, I don't see anything '*lucky*' about the accident. Not only am I in excruciating pain, but I lost the only family I had. I couldn't even attend my grandfather's funeral. *Lucky* is not the word I would have chosen."

After gathering her composure she apologized, "I'm sorry Doctor. I know you didn't mean it like that. I didn't mean to take it out on you."

"I understand and I'm sorry too," Dr. Jenkins told her, "I didn't mean to come across as abrupt or to sound insensitive. I just wanted to make the point that you have a whole future ahead of you. Ms. Summers, I'm very sorry about your grandfather. I'm quite aware of all you've been through. I think you're a real strong person. If ever I was in a situation like yours, I would hope someone like you would be there to help see me through."

◊ ◊ ◊

"Annie, are you sure you don't want to go inside," Naomi asked, trying to persuade her, "you really need to rest."

"I'm okay. Besides, the cool air feels good on my face. Funny how one single event can change more than one life. You would have been on Barbados, living out your retirement years in your native country."

"Yeah, I know. I was considering retiring after taking care of your grandfather. But when this happened to you, I couldn't leave. I think I would have been hurt if you had not asked me to stay with you. This is where I belong. Talk about changes. Look at what that accident did to you. It compromised your health and ruined your career."

"I never once thought about losing it all, Naomi. Not like this. One day my face is on the covers of all the fashion magazines and now, no one is interested in me. Even after all these surgeries my face is still scarred and disfigured. Maybe someday I'll feel good about myself and not have to wear my hair so as to cover the right side of my face."

"Annie, ever since your release from the hospital you have shunned every form of publicity. You're embarrassed of your appearance and have become a recluse. I know that you needed the time to physically heal and time to work through the psychological scars caused by that accident, but there's a world out there that is part of you as much as you are part of it. You can't hide on this farm forever."

"Oh, Naomi, If only it was that easy. I'm so afraid of how the public will react to my scarred face. And what if I never find that special someone who will accept me for who I am, regardless of what I look like?"

"Annie, my sweet angel, you have got to accept the fact that the Angelika of the runway no longer exists. In my country, beauty comes from within. You have a beautiful and loving heart. Don't deprive yourself of the wonderful experience of sharing your life with others just because of what you look like on the outside. Yes, people will stare, but once they get to know you they'll see your heart, not your face. There's someone out there for you. You two will meet at the right time and place. Annie, I'm starting to shiver from this cool weather. I'm going inside."

"And I'll be out here," teased Annie, "All by my lonesome self; just me, my mug of tea, and a dark abyss that's harboring an unknown creature."

"Oh please Annie, spare me the melodrama," Naomi laughed as she joked with her. "I'll only be a few feet from here. I'll be that woman wrapped in a warm sofa throw. You know, the one watching our favorite cooking show? . . . That will be *moi*."

◦ ◦ ◦

It was Saturday night and Derrick was at the movie theater when his pager vibrated. *Just my luck,* he thought, *twenty minutes before the end of the movie and I get called.*

"Hate to bother you, but they need you to go in," the answering service notified Derrick when he responded to the page.

Rushing back to work, he decided to take a short cut through a road that bypassed all the traffic lights. *I've taken this road many times,* he recalled, *at this time of night there'll hardly be any traffic.* He floored the pedal of his European sports car and smiled as the engine purred with delight.

Derrick maneuvered his way through a few miles of winding road and was racing down a long stretch of paved country road when a loud explosion broke the peaceful silence of the night. He fought to keep the car under control and slowly pulled over, off the road, coming to a complete stop next to a wooded area.

He called on his cell phone to let them know, "I've had a blowout. It'll take me a few minutes to change the tire. I'll be there shortly."

At first the cool damp air felt invigorating. But after a few seconds, out in the open, he started getting bitten by night bugs. *If I would have known I'd be changing a tire on a foggy country road, I would've worn long pants,* Derrick thought swatting off the insects.

He was in the middle of changing the flat when a truck with three guys stopped next to him. "Need any help?" they called out.

"I think I've got it. Thanks, anyway," he responded, as the good Samaritans drove off.

He caught a glimpse of their personalized license plate, BORN2DIE. *Man*, he thought, *ain't that the truth.*

After changing the tire and placing the jack and flat in the trunk, Derrick looked up and saw the same guys returning. They jumped out of their white truck and started small talk as they approached him.

"Sure you don't need help?" the driver asked.

"Nice car. What year is it?" another questioned Derrick, running his hand over the body of the sports car.

"Do you live nearby?" the third guy inquired.

Sensing that the guys were not there for a friendly, social visit, Derrick started toward the door. "I'm really in quite a hurry. I'm on my way to work," he said, trying to sound polite.

As he reached for the door handle he felt a sharp blow to the back of the head. One of the guys slammed him against the car and another held him up while they worked him over.

"You don't understand," they told him as they delivered several punches to his rib cage. "We really like your ride. Hope you don't mind us borrowing it."

The men were relentless in beating their defenseless victim. After he slumped down to the ground, they took turns kicking his face and body. He could faintly hear their laughter through the ringing in his ears. His entire body and head were throbbing with pain. He was outnumbered, had very little strength, and at this point knew that fighting back was not an option. He had to get away from these guys before they killed him.

When their attention turned to their intended prize, Derrick took advantage of the moment. He mustered up what little strength he had left and darted toward the wooded area.

"Look at him run. Can't even standup," they taunted him while laughing and yelling obscenities.

With one eye completely shut and a small slit in the other, he stumbled through the thick brush. Branches and thorny vines slapped and cut into his face and body as he evaded his tormentors.

Gotta get away. Gotta get away, he repeatedly told himself as he escaped the tormenters. *The deeper I travel into these woods, the more distance I can get between me and those guys.*

The adrenaline rush brought on by the fear that the assailants were still in pursuit was beginning to wear off. Struggling to distant his mutilated body from his attackers, Derrick found himself traveling entirely on all fours.

Every bone and muscle in his body throbbed with pain. The disoriented and completely spent body of a once physically fit being suddenly felt the sensation of numbness as it drifted into unconsciousness.

Derrick's face was virtually unrecognizable. His entire body was bloodied and swollen. His shoulder length hair was matted with blood, sweat, and debris from the brush he had trampled through. His chest, arms, legs, and hands were cut, bruised, and bleeding. Looking more like a creature out of a B-rated horror movie, the pulverized and exhausted form, slowly fall on its side.

◻ ◻ ◻

Annie had been sitting motionless, breaking her pose only to take a sip from the refilled mug Naomi returned with. The sound of snapping branches immediately brought her thoughts back to her front porch duties. She firmly gripped the rifle and squinted focusing her 20/20 eye vision in the direction of the approaching beast of prey.

"Come on out," she whispered, "I've been waiting for you."

"Do you see it?" she asked Naomi, still trying to get a visual on the creature.

It's probably that large red fox spotted by the local farmers or maybe even the elusive cougar that's been creating havoc in the tri-county area, Annie tried to figure out what it was she was about to face.

Sensing danger, the entire hen house and the miniature goats started getting restless and agitated. The noisy animals slightly distracted Annie, but she regained her poise, and concentrated solely on what was coming out of the woods. "They know it's coming," she whispered to Naomi.

They caught a glimpse of the culprit as it emerged out of the thick brush. It was low to the ground creeping in stealth like manner. Snorting and audibly wheezing the dark shadow appeared.

Annie rose up from her chair, slowly and quietly. *Alright Annie,* she thought to herself, *be careful not to frighten off the creature.* Naomi silently stood behind her. Like a sentry alerted by the advancement of the enemy, Annie too, was prepared to do battle.

The silhouette of the tall slender figure against the faint background of a misty moonlight, with her rifle aimed in the direction of the invader, would have made, in better times, the front covers of nearly every magazine in print. But that was her life as Angelika, when every move and every second of her life was sought by the paparazzi and her fans.

Her life, now drastically changed, was mundane and of no interest to the world that once worshipped her. Tonight, Annie, the private individual was protecting her property. With diligence and purpose in mind, she stood with her rifle trained in the direction of the unknown foe and patiently waited for just the right moment. "Come on baby. Come to Mama," she whispered.

"I see it," Annie announced, "it's coming towards us."

One chance, one shot, she recalled her grandfather coaching her as he passed on the skills of a true marksman. She inhaled the cool brisk air and briefly held her breath. Slowly and deliberately her long slender finger pulled back on the trigger. The loud, thunderous boom produced by the gunshot made Naomi jump and seemed to echo across the sky as the sound waves reverberated off the trunks of the tall pine and oak trees.

Recognizing the screams of an injured cougar, they said in unison, "It's the mountain lion."

Grabbing the flashlight, Naomi shone it in the direction of the cat. Together, they cautiously approached the cougar. Fatally wounded, they saw it wobble unsteadily and then collapse. One hundred and eighty pounds lay lifeless on the damp ground.

"Sure is a large cat," said Annie.

"Make that a large, dead cat," Naomi corrected her.

While Annie was poking the fallen beast of prey with her rifle, a second creature came crashing out of the woods.

"WATCH OUT! THERE'S ANOTHER ONE!" yelled Naomi.

Annie hurriedly aimed the rifle in the direction of the second beast and made her shot. The creature slowly fell on its side, splashing onto the pool of the dead cougar's blood.

The second animal was stirring and softly gurgling through a larynx full of blood. Naomi turned the flashlight on it. The two women were shocked to see that it was a human being. The man's face was severely beaten. His eyes were swollen shut and countless of bloody gashes and welts crisscrossed his face and entire body. He cargo pocket shorts and shirt were in shreds and he was missing a shoe. His breathing was shallow as he gasped for air.

"I shot a man," Annie hysterically cried, "I shot a man."

"I'll call 911", Naomi shouted, running back to the house.

"Don't worry, I'll stay with you until help arrives," Annie tried comforting the wounded man.

Holding him close, she could feel the irregular deformities of his broken skeletal bones. *It's a miracle he's still alive,* she thought. She laid him down and covered him with the blanket she had been wearing. The man's blood mingled on the ground with that of the dead cat's. His head was cradled on Annie's lap as he slowly bled from all his open wounds. His body shivered uncontrollably.

"I'm sorry. I'm so sorry," sobbed Annie, "I thought you were a cougar."

Naomi returned with two more blankets and some sheets. She tore the sheets into strips and commenced dressing the wounds. They did the best they could to keep him warm and to shield him from the damp ground.

Sirens could be heard in the far distance.

◦ ◦ ◦

Derrick survived the beatings. His face, however, was permanently scarred. None of his wounds were caused by a gunshot. Annie's shot missed him as he started to fall to the ground.

It took several weeks for him to recover. During that time Annie and Derrick developed a close relationship. She helped him deal with the psychological trauma and was there to give him encouragement and support throughout his reconstructive surgeries.

Dr. Derrick Jenkins and Annie later married and honeymooned in Barbados, where they visited their retired friend, Naomi.

FAMILY PHOTOS

*Under contract to the Orient they flew,
to work in education, the two
enjoyed the fiesta, good food, and new friends,
don't tell me this story ain't true.*

—R. Quero

Family Photos

Arriving at their final destination, Jerold Furgusson and Nancy Metler found themselves in front of the Manila International Airport, trying to flag down a cab. They were in for a very interesting and educational experience in the Philippine Islands. The hot tropical sun coupled with the high humidity was immediately felt by the two travellers. People walked to and fro carrying umbrellas to shield themselves from the sun and using hand-made fans to help cool them off. A vast number of the Filipinos walked around covering their noses with handkerchiefs or wearing face masks to keep from inhaling the city smog, generated by unregulated vehicle exhaust.

There were loud horns, and constant beeping of cars, jeeps, and motorbikes. The ringing of bicycle bells, alerting pedestrians of their presence, went virtually unnoticed by the hurried citizens. The chatter from the throngs of pedestrians drowned out the whistles by policemen trying to keep the heavy traffic flowing smoothly. All these urban sounds bounced off the walls of buildings, making them sound louder and more chaotic.

"Welcome to the Philippines, Nancy," Jerold said, removing his sunglasses and rubbing his irritated eyes. "I haven't been here since 1982 when I was in the Air Force. Some things just never change."

"It smells really good," Nancy commented, as she took in the aroma of the food being prepared by street vendors.

Jerold purchased a couple of food items that resembled long Chinese spring rolls. "These are *lumpias,*" he said giving one to Nancy. "They're stuffed with meat and veggies and then deep fried."

"They're delicious," she said between bites. "It sure does hit the spot."

"I was starting to get a little hunger myself," Jerold agreed, licking his fingers.

"Come on, let's grab that jeepney," Jerold said pointing and moving in the direction of a festive decorated jeep that had just pulled up to the curb.

"*Mabuhay,*" greeted the driver in *Tagalog*, the national dialect of the Philippines, "Hello, where like go?" he asked, with his thick Filipino accent.

"Can you take us to the Clark Industrial Complex?" Jerold asked.

"You mean Clark Business Park and Resort, new name, change in March, new name. Yes can take," the driver said, as he started loading their luggage onto the roof of the vehicle.

"Yes Clark Business Park and Resort, I think. Outside Angeles City, right?" Jerold asked, making sure they were speaking of the same place.

"Oh yes, same place, different name. Clark Business Park and Resort," the jeepney owner repeated himself, trying hard not to lose a customer.

"Okay, good. Do you take American dollars?"

"Yes, dollars OK," the driver responded, grateful for a fare that would make him some extra cash.

"Hot today. Very hot today," he pointed out, as he wiped the sweat off his forehead. "You from New York City? Los Angeles? Or maybe Texas?" he asked, sharing his knowledge on US geography.

"No, we're from Mississippi. Have you ever heard of that state?" Jerold answered him, as the two sweaty and tired Americans climbed into the rear of the jeepney and sat on two bench seats opposite each other.

"Oh yes, I know. Mississippi River," the driver said, while loading the remainder of the bags into the front seat.

"These sure are nifty looking taxis," Nancy commented, observing the dozens of similar, but unique vehicles on the busy boulevard.

"The jeepney is a throwback to small WWII Japanese trucks that resembled jeeps," explained Jerold, "they were used to transport supplies and troops during the war. Some of the original trucks might still exist but new jeepneys are being manufactured to serve strictly as open air urban taxis."

Theirs was painted bright yellow with red and green diamonds. It was extremely ornate with chrome and colorful banners.

All hopes for having the jeepney to themselves were soon shattered when the driver made a stop to pick up other passengers. At the next stop a man climbed aboard the crowded transport carrying a bamboo cage full of chickens. Another had a goat that kept eating away at a lady's bundle of green produce. It fazed no one when a young couple got on with a squealing piglet. "It's all taken in stride, just another day going home from the market place," Jerold, a camera buff, commented as he kept shooting away, taking pictures of anything and everything.

"Take a picture of me," Nancy called across to Jerold. The piglet had rested its head on her lap and was snorting in its sleep.

Their fellow passengers laughed along with the foreign travelers. An embarrassed, young lady pulled the pig off and timidly apologized to Nancy. "So sorry, forgive," she spoke with broken English.

It took over an hour just to get out of the city limits. Manila, as does Seoul, Korea or any other Asian capital comes across as a chaotic congestion of metal carnage, especially to the first time visitor.

"A three-lane street in Manila is usually flowing four lanes of traffic and a two-lane is normally turned into a three-lane road. Side streets are notorious for traffic jams created by impatient vehicle operators weaving their way through the lines of slow moving traffic," Jerold shared. "I've always enjoyed this facet of large foreign cities," he said. "Look at how close these cars, buses, and trucks all cram in together, just mere fractions of an inch from scraping up against each other. We're in a real open air taxi. Riding with no windows or sides from our waists to the roof of this jeepney really lends to the experience of being in a crowded Asian city. Look, I can literally reach out and touch the car next to us."

"I'm trying hard to appreciate this wonderful feeling you're getting high on," Nancy said, looking a little sickly. "But all this exhaust is making me a little nauseous."

"Hang in there Nancy. We'll soon be out of the city and into some fresh country air."

Relief for Nancy and the other passengers came only when their jeepney finally cleared the city limits and hit the open country on a road named

"McArthur Highway". Laden with a full load of passengers, luggage, farm animals, and wrapped packages from the market, the colorful transport slowly but steadily kept its course. The short forty mile ride, would however, take a long two hours.

"I think the Philippines' countryside is beautiful. It's picturesque, refreshing, and virtually smog free," Nancy made her appreciation of the countryside be known.

"I agree. It certainly is pleasant out here," Jerold said, nodding his head.

At this time of day there seemed to be very little traffic. An occasional vehicle easily zipped past the weighted down jeepney, leaving them in a cloud of colorful exhaust fumes and dust.

Thirty minutes out of the city, a passenger yelled something in the native dialect and the driver pulled over to the side of the road. Several of the riders jumped off and ran into the field. The men turned their backs to the road and proceeded to urinate. Two women also went out there and facing away from the jeepney, squatted down to do their thing.

"I don't know about you Jerold, but I've gotta go."

Nancy's full bladder beckoned her to a nearby banyan tree, where she too, did her business. Jerold simply turned and looked the other direction, pretending to be occupied with taking pictures of the piglet and the goat nibbling on the unattended vegetables.

Not one to easily get embarrassed, Nancy climbed back into the jeepney and simply said, "When in Rome, do as the Romans do."

Shortly after getting back on their trek, the driver decided to pass a slow moving cart being pulled by a team of *carabaos*. As he was passing the farmer, a large brown bus (affectionately called *the Hare*) was rapidly approaching from the opposite direction. Neither driver showed signs of backing down.

Above the loud strain of the jeepney's motor, Nancy could be heard screaming, "OH MY GOD. WE ARE GONNA GET KILLED."

The Filipinos laughed loudly, enjoying the spectacle of her fear and the thrill of the daredevils' challenge. "No die. No die. Jeepney driver good," they assured her.

After just barely clearing the cart and the native water buffalos of the Philippines, the jeepney pulled back onto the right lane. Within seconds *the Hare* barreled past them causing the smaller vehicle to rock back and forth. By the time they emerged from a large cloud of dust, the bus had long vanished.

Although this sort of hazardous driving did not particularly bother any of the locals, Nancy, a newbie to the Philippines, was slow to recover from her first "hare racing" experience.

"That, I think, I would classify as exhilarating," Jerold said. "Definitely more fun than a roller coaster ride."

"Well, I'm glad I emptied my bladder earlier. Otherwise, I think I'd be sitting in a puddle. Please tell me this isn't the norm."

"Don't worry Nancy. You'll have plenty of time to get used to the driving habits of the Filipino people."

During the remainder of the ride to Clark, Jerold shared with Nancy, "I wasn't the first Furgusson to set foot on Philippine soil. I had a granduncle, from my dad's side who supposedly served as a missionary throughout Southeast Asia. He eventually ended up in the Philippine Islands during WWII. He made the Orient his life's project and never returned to the States. I only knew him through the many stories dad used to tell me about 'Uncle Bernie' and his travels."

"It wasn't until the 1980's that I spent time on Clark. I was assigned to the 7007th Airborne Command and Control Squadron. We would stop here for a couple of nights of crew rest before continuing on our missions. Most of the time, we were billeted off base. It gave me the chance to get acquainted with the surrounding community and the Filipino culture."

"Other than what you've told me about this Clark place, do you know much more about it," Nancy asked.

"I'm sure it too is not the same as when I used to fly in and out of Clark Air Base before *Mount Pinatubo* erupted in 1991. The disaster destroyed the air base and most of the surrounding towns. Prior to that, Clark was the largest American controlled air base outside of the United States. After the volcano erupted, the base was handed over to the Philippine government," Jerold told her.

"What condition is it in now?" inquired Nancy.

"The volcano's destructive force destroyed all landmarks and dramatically changed or completely obliterated much of the beautiful countryside. Luckily, nature grew back most of the jungles and green pastures. All the buildings currently standing are either redone or are all new. My old stomping grounds are not as I remember them. For all practical purposes, it's like visiting the place for the first time," Jerold told his traveling companion.

"It took the Philippine government a few years to clean up the volcanic mess, but they have turned it into a highly profitable industrial complex with an international airport, golf resort, and cultural center. The new educational facility, which we'll be working at, is considered state of the art and unrivaled worldwide."

The two American educators were in the Philippines to help the government start a Center for Autism, an extension to the special education programs already in place.

Jerold had received a call asking him to consider coming out of retirement and serving in the capacity of consultant and coordinator for the implementation the new project. His many years in the field of special education and experience in helping to implement similar programs in the United States made him the prime choice for the position. The assignment required him to sign a one-year contract, with salaries being paid directly from the Philippine's Educational System Fund.

"Well, I'm glad you considered me as your assistant. Coming out of retirement was a no-brainer. You know how much I like to travel and how much I loved working in the classroom. How could I have passed up the opportunity?"

"With your experience in special education and our prior working relationship, it just seemed like the right team for this job," Jerold replied. "Knowing your passion for traveling and visiting new places, I planned our arrival a few days early so we could do some sightseeing before we started work."

▫ ▫ ▫

The newly built center was quite impressive. It consisted of two multi-story buildings. The main building was made up of administrative offices, classrooms, conference rooms, and an auditorium. The second building housed the dormitory rooms, cafeteria, laundry, recreation center, library, and a gym.

The land, donated by the local government, was located adjacent to the Clark Business Park and Resort. The facilities and the operational expenses were being finance by the International Council for Autism, a non-profit organization.

Jerold's and Nancy's home for the next twelve months was located at the golf resort about one-half hour from the Center. Each was provided a large two-bedroom condo, on the golf course, overlooking a ten acre, man-made lake.

"Not bad. We should have gone into the consultant business years ago," quipped Nancy.

◻ ◻ ◻

After settling into their accommodations, they contacted their sponsor and spent time getting acquainted with the personnel assigned as their teaching staff.

That evening they caught up on some much needed sleep and rest.

The next morning they asked the resort's activity coordinator for suggestions on how to spend their first full day in the Philippines.

"It's spring time and there many fiestas in progress. There's one just a few kilometers from here," the young lady behind the desk informed them. "It's a twenty kilometer taxi ride, over unpaved back roads, a little bumpy and dusty, but I think you'll find the festival well worth the ride."

They arrived at the village about 11:30 A.M. The fiesta was in full swing. The large crowd was comprised of locals, tourists, and residents from neighboring towns. The entire village was decorated with colorful banners, balloons, and streamers. In the center of the village several large pits were excavated and contained a pig, a cow, a goat, or chickens all being roasted over an open flame. Festival goers were invited to just walk up to the pits and slice off a piece of meat. Also available was *lumpia*, a noodle dish called *pancit* (similar to Chinese *lo mein* or Japanese *yaki soba*), and various vegetable and fish dishes. All side dishes and cold drinks were on tables outside shops and private homes. Folding chairs and benches were placed throughout the town square for folks to sit, eat, rest, or just enjoy the entertainment. The food, refreshments, and entertainment were all free. Throughout the day, music was provided by small bands and traditional Filipino dances were performed by local dance troupes.

Jerold and Nancy graciously helped themselves to the food being offered. They made their way to a couple of unoccupied chairs, located on the front row, facing the main stage. Their seats were next to a family of six.

"Hi, I'm Jim", spoke up the gentleman. "And this is my wife Marta and our four children."

"Nice to meet you," replied Jerold, offering Jim a firm hand shake. "My name is Jerold and this is Nancy, my friend and co-worker."

The children quickly took a liking to Nancy and competed for the honor of holding her hand.

"Children don't be a nuisance," their mother scolded.

"Oh that's all right, Marta. I love children," Nancy let her know, playfully ruffling the children's hair.

"What is it that brings you to the Philippines?" inquired Jim.

Jim and his wife were very friendly and genuinely interested in the information regarding the Center for Autism.

"My husband and I were also teachers. We taught school in the local villages. We concentrated on reading, math, and conversational English. Most of our students were first through fourth grade," Marta shared.

They enjoyed themselves sharing stories and eating. "Look Nancy, I made those pork *lumpias,* over there in the long pan. You and Jerold try some," Marta proudly pointed out her contribution to the fiesta. "Our family comes to these fiestas about twice a year. We enjoy the festivities, the food, and the new friends we encounter."

Marta and Nancy quickly became friends and spent a considerable amount of time talking about the difference in fashion, food, and the educational system.

"Children behave. Don't crowd Ms. Nancy," Marta kept reminding them as they argued over who sat next to the teacher from America.

Jim was more interested in how things were going on in the States. Like many Americans, he made the Philippines his home and had not been back to the States in years. He and Jerold spoke extensively about politics and sports.

"Gosh, it's nice to be able to have a conversation with another American. Jerold tell me more about your family. Do you have many siblings? Are you a close knit family? Are your parents still living? Jim asked. "I do hope you don't think I'm prying. One of my interests is learning about the difference in families, specifically the impact the unit, known as the family, has on its individual members. You see, one of my degrees was in the field of sociology."

During their conversation, the two men walked around the plaza as Jerold took pictures. When they returned to the ladies and the kids, Jerold busied himself with setting up the tripod in preparation for a group shot.

"What are you doing?" Jim asked, stepping away from the view of the camera.

"I'm getting my equipment ready to take a picture of all of us together," Jerold responded. "I hope you don't mind if I snap a picture of your family."

"You mean a picture of all of us? Me too?"

"Why of course, Jim. You too."

"I don't like to take pictures," Jim said shaking his head.

"Come on don't be shy. It will be a nice memory of our day together," pled Jerold.

"Yes Jim. Let's take a picture. It's nothing Jim. It's all right. It's really nothing," Marta tried encouraging her husband. "You and I can stand next to Jerold and I know the kids would love to sit next to Nancy."

"Well okay," Jim finally agreed, after Nancy took him by the arm and led him to a nearby bench.

The four children were excited about the photo shoot and were vying for position on Nancy's lap. A petite lady, Nancy was only able to hold one child on her lap.

The camera was on the tripod, so all Jerold needed to do was set it on automatic. He ran and stood between Jim and Marta, who were standing directly behind Nancy and the kids.

"Say cheese," Jerold and Jim simultaneously told the group, as the camera snapped the shot.

"One more," Jerold called out as he ran back to reset the timer. He rushed back in time to wrap his arms around both Jim and Marta. "Everyone smile."

After three and a half hours of taking in the festivities, Nancy asked, "Does anyone want to explore the rest of this small village?"

"Yes, I think I do," Jerold answered. "Anyone else want to join us?"

Jim and Marta chose to stay and watch the festivities. "Thanks, but we've seen the shops already."

The little shops were quaint and filled with many interesting crafts made by local artisans.

"I love these neat trinkets and the handmade jewelry. And look at this beautiful lace work," Nancy pointed out.

They went in and out of several shops and then came across a small museum. In it were the archives for the province of *Pampanga* in which the small town was located. There were official records, correspondence, and documents from every government that at one time ruled or controlled that area of the Philippines.

"Look," Jerold pointed out, "This display of artifacts dates back a few hundred years." The surrounding walls were covered with pictures of dignitaries, common everyday people, and events that made *Pampanga* the province that it is today.

"Check out these before and after pictures of the province following the volcano's eruption. This little town was miraculously spared the destructive force Mother Nature dealt during that horrific week," Nancy pointed out.

While Jerold was reading about the many dialects spoken throughout the Philippines and the country's struggle to unite all the provinces with the use of one national dialect, Nancy called out, "Come see this. The people in this old photo closely resemble Jim and his family."

Under the faded black and white picture the label read, "P#1583 Missionary and family, circa 1943". Next to the family picture was a separate photo of the four children labeled "P#1584 Missionary's Children."

Jerold studied the picture and agreed that the family and that of the children closely resembled their new friends. He wrote down the reference numbers and asked the curator if he had further information on those particular pictures.

The curator brought out a large journal in which all the entries were handwritten. He pointed to the recorded data and read the information out loud, "Item P#1583, circa 1943. James Bernard Furgusson, wife, and children. Missionary and schoolmaster."

"I can't believe it", exclaimed Jerold, "This is my Granduncle Bernie."

"The next entry", the curator continued," P# 1584, circa 1943. Missionary's Children. Rudy, Sam, Prichard, and Perry Furgusson."

"Wow. And these are Uncle Bernie's children. Our new friends and I are probably related in some way," an excited Jerold said. "We're probably first or second cousins. Let's see if they're still at the fiesta," he called back to Nancy, as he led the way out the door.

Exiting the museum they found the streets nearly cleared of most fiesta goers. It was evening and the festivities were winding down. Their friends were nowhere in sight.

Before returning to the condos, Jerold had the taxi driver stop at a local store, where film was processed and printed. He was excited about the pictures and tracking down Jim and his family.

"If we're related," Jerold told Nancy, "Jim might be able to shed some light on Uncle Bernie and his life in the Philippines. Gosh, I can't wait to tell Dad about this."

The next day he picked up the photos and was pleasantly pleased with the vibrant colors. "Just look at these," he said showing Nancy the pictures, "the candid expressions of the Filipino people are great."

As a freelance photographer, he always aimed for the best in picture taking. The shots of the farmers working the rice fields with the grass huts in the background were definitely travel magazine material. And the pictures of the loaded down jeepney were priceless. He rapidly thumbed through the photos, eager to see the ones taken at the fiesta.

"They all turned out great," Nancy said, as Jerold handed her the pictures. "The colorful banners, the graceful dancers, and the cheerful crowd will all be great pictures for your portfolio."

Looking at the last of the pictures, they couldn't believe what they were seeing. One picture was of Nancy sitting alone with her empty arms extended outward over her lap and Jerold standing alone, behind her. The second picture had Nancy in a similar pose with Jerold standing behind her, both his arms stretched out, as if wrapped around someone's shoulder on either side.

"Nancy," Jerold finally said, with an eerie tone in his voice, "I think . . . I think yesterday we met my Uncle Bernie."

HOBO JUNGLE

*The weather was foggy and damp,
when the customer dressed-up as a tramp,
robbed the bank of its money, slipped away from
authorities, but later was caught at the camp.*

—*R. Quero*

Hobo Jungle

It was a damp foggy afternoon in the City of Ventura, California. Customers had been filing in and out of Central City Bank all day in costumes and makeup.

"I love Halloween," Sheila ghoulishly announced to her co-worker manning the next window. "I think I enjoy it just as much as the kids."

"Me too," the bank teller answered, "and I'm so glad the heavy rains have stopped. It would've ruined it for the kids."

Waiting in line for the next available teller was a rabbit, a cowboy, and a spaceman.

"Next in line please," Sheila called out.

"Hi, the life size pink bunny said, "I'm sure glad it's Friday. I can't wait to get home. I have a lot to do before the party. Are you still planning on coming?"

"I'm looking forward to it, Carla. Love the rabbit outfit. Do you want your paycheck deposited into your savings? Sheila asked.

"It took me two weeks to sew this costume. I think it turned out pretty good. Yeah, put half of my check into the savings account and give me the rest in cash. I need to pay some bills on my way home."

"Next," Sheila called out. *Just forty minutes 'til closing,* she thought glancing at the clock.

Within the next half hour, the steady flow of bank customers slowly dwindled. Except for the man in a tramp's outfit the lobby was empty. It was about a minute before closing time and he made it to the window just in the nick of time.

The man, in dirty, tattered clothes nonchalantly announced in a heavy southern drawl, "I want to make a withdrawal," and slid a note across the window toward her.

Sheila's eyes widen as she read the note, 'This is a robbery. If I hear any alarms or screaming, I will shoot everyone'.

"Put all the money you can stuff into this canvas bag," he demanded, "and don't forget the cash in the vault."

Bill, the manager, had just finished locking the front door, and drawing the floor length drapes across the front windows. He and Sheila were the only two employees left to lock up the bank that afternoon.

"You," the robber ordered Bill, "Get behind the counter and lie face down on the floor. If either of you tries to be a hero, you'll be a dead hero," the robber threatened.

Sheila handed the man the full bag. He then placed the bag in his brown leather suitcase. The vagabond locked the two bank workers in the vault before exiting through the back door that led out into an alleyway. The security camera recorded him walking down the alley and simply disappearing into the dense fog.

◘ ◘ ◘

Located sixty miles north of Los Angeles, the City of Ventura, in the 1960's, was a quiet coastal community. Hobos, at that time, still traversed the Southern California counties, courtesy of the rail system. Located at the mouth of the Ventura River, where the fresh water emptied into the Pacific Ocean was a site affectionately called 'Hobo Jungle'. It consisted of several acres, nicely tucked away, surrounded by fresh water streams. The river split, creating the streams, which in turn formed an isle, before mixing with the ocean's salt water. A few yards north of this lush wooded area was a bridge that spanned over the river, carrying the freight trains that vagabonds frequently rode. As the trains slowed down to navigate the bend leading into the city limits, the boxcar riders easily jumped off and on at their leisure. For many poor wayfaring strangers this tranquil municipality was a popular place to layover, with 'Hobo Jungle' a favorite site to set up camp for the night.

◘ ◘ ◘

The bank robber changed clothes and stuffed them into the brown case. He made sure no one was watching and buried the suitcase in a secluded part of the wooded area. He washed the makeup off at a nearby stream and returned to make sure he could remember where he stashed the cash.

One hundred and ninety five steps from the buried treasure to the foot of the bridge. A direct shot, due south from the bridge to the spot marked "X", he greedily laughed as he made a mental note of the exact site.

Climbing an embankment constructed of boulders, he got up onto the railroad tracks. *If I'm stopped and questioned, I'll just say I'm taking a walk along the tracks,* he thought to himself. Halfway across the bridge he heard the train whistle blowing as it came around the bend. As he started to run his foot missed the railroad tie and his leg went all the way through, dangling underneath the bridge. With the remainder of his body exposed to the oncoming tonnage of moving steel, the man's screams were drowned out by the roar of the locomotive's engines. He could see the engineer looking the other direction, enjoying the sunset.

Feeling his entire body vibrate as the approaching train rattled the bridge, he laid his lean body as flat as possible. "Lord, this is it. Forgive me. I guess crime doesn't pay," he prayed out loud as the train rolled over him.

◘ ◘ ◘

At 7:00 P.M. Sam received a call at home. "Detective Stone, the Central City Bank was robbed this afternoon," Chief Lofton said over the telephone. "I'm switching out personnel and I want you to represent the department as the senior detective from the department. The local FBI office has been notified. They'll be in charge of the investigation and we'll provide any assistance they may need. Agent Cruz will meet you at the bank."

The detective reached the bank first. "Hi Mickey," he greeted the agent who arrived half an hour later. "I see you're limping too. What happened to you?"

"Twisted my ankle hiking up to Ventura's twin trees," the agent replied, "What about you?"

"I went fishing at 'the Rincon' today, you know, between here and Santa Barbara. I caught three large yellow mouth perch. Lost my footing climbing up the slope from the beach," Sam said laughing at their clumsiness.

"By the way Mick, I saw you a few weeks ago in the play *The Circus Clowns*. I read the great reviews it received. You certainly seem to enjoy acting. All that makeup must really irritate your skin. How long have you been involved in acting?"

"Yeah, it's a lot of fun. I've been acting since college. It's my passion. "You want to work this as a team? Last time we shared all the information we were able to crack the case pretty fast. We all received kudos for working together," Mickey said, quickly changing the subject and getting down to the business of investigating.

Sam filled his federal counterpart in on information his police officers had already gathered from the bank employees. "Looks like some guy dressed up as a tramp and came trick or treating. When they felt sure the thief was gone, the employees called using a phone in the vault."

"We've dusted for prints, but the thief wore gloves as part of his costume. No one from the neighboring businesses saw or heard anything. He escaped out the back," Sam briefed the agent.

"I'll have my guys view the film again. They might be able to see something your guys missed. We'll also interview the manager and teller again," the federal agent said. "What about the bank guard?" he asked Sam.

"This small bank never hired a guard."

"It's seems like quite an easy robbery. I'm beginning to smell a possible inside job," Mickey commented.

"Yeah, that thought did cross my mind. But I've known of Bill and Sheila for quite a while, I don't think they fit the profile. They both have stable family lives and are quite involved in the local community. I doubt if either would do this sort of thing."

"I know. But we still need to check if either is in deep financial trouble. You know, just a routine check. We also need to find out who they have been associating with the past few weeks or months. See if your department can get some phone records. My office will investigate their financial backgrounds," Agent Cruz said.

"And I'll have my officers comb the entire alley again and re-check the dumpsters and trash cans."

The next morning Sam and Mickey met for coffee. Both the police department and the FBI had been working the case all night.

"As of this morning, this is pretty much a cold case," Mickey said, sipping on his coffee.

"The guy apparently knew what he was doing. A quiet entrance followed by a swift exit. Heck, for all we know he's probably in another county or state by now. Might have even been a real hobo, in disguise, and hopped a train out of here."

They both laughed. "Pretty funny, huh? A hobo made up as a hobo. I love that one," Mickey said, choking on his coffee. "Hey, maybe you have something there," he said jumping up and heading toward the door. "Take care of the tab Sam. I heard you got a raise because of our last case together. I'll be in the car making a couple of calls to my guys."

Mickey was wrapping up a call on the car phone when Sam climbed into the driver's seat. I've got my guys going to the train depot. Maybe someone will remember seeing a man with that suitcase," he said handing Sam a copy of blown up pictures. "This is really the only lead we have; an unidentifiable tramp carrying a brown case."

"I had a couple of officers check out the bus station yesterday," Sam mentioned, "told them to ask if anyone with a southern accent passed through there. Not very many southerners come through here. He'd stick out like a sore thumb."

"Forgot about that," Mickey thought out loud, as he reached for the phone to call his G-men, to remind them of the accent.

"Sam, let's go check out Hobo Jungle," suggested the agent.

They drove west on Main Street in a new, white, unmarked police car. "Nice car Sam. Read in the paper where this is the first of the fleet of twenty-four V-8 engines your department is getting."

"Yeah, it's a beauty. Chief gave me the keys a week ago. He doesn't like it. Claims it's too much power for him," Sam told Mickey as he turned left on Meta Street and headed toward the fairgrounds.

'Hobo Jungle' was a short walk from the stables, which were located behind the grandstands on the west side of the fairgrounds. The strong smell of fresh manure filled the air and they had to sidestep piles of dung while cutting across the green pasture.

"I never liked hanging around horses and this is why," Sam said with disgust, as he pulled his foot out of a fresh pile. "Think we'll find anything here, besides horse crap?"

"Not really looking for anything. Just hoping someone might recognize our guy in the picture."

The two walked through the woods stopping only to ask the vagrants if they had seen anyone or anything depicted in the photo.

From the corner of their eyes they caught a glimpse of a shady looking character. Every time Sam or Mickey looked his way, the homeless man looked away.

"I'll speak with that one Mickey. You see if anyone around here has seen or heard anything."

The hobo stood up to leave. "Wait up my friend," Sam called out. "I just want to ask some questions."

"Just have a seat where you are." Sam introduced himself as Mickey walked deeper into the woods. "What's your name stranger?"

"Todd, the hobo answered.

Sam's conversation with Todd faded as Mickey got further away.

Mickey spoke with another homeless man that seemed to be in a hurry to leave. "Hey, buddy where were you going in such a rush?"

"I was getting ready to hop the next freight," the old man said.

"How long have you been hanging around here," Mickey asked him.

"Set up camp late last night. I stop off here to rest and bath in the stream whenever I'm in town," the homeless man replied.

"You didn't happen to see anything unusual or someone in a hobo outfit? Did you?"

"Mister everyone who stops off here wears a hobo outfit. That's what we are. There are a few acres of woods here and most the time we just keep to ourselves, unless we're sharing coffee or stories. The guys I saw last night were regulars to the 'jungle'. I didn't see anything unusual."

The team spent another hour and a half on the wooded isle interviewing several other men. "I'll meet you back at the car, I'm going to talk to that Todd guy again," Sam said.

"There's something about that Todd. Can't quite put my finger on it," Mickey told Sam when they were both in the car again. "Did you find out anything else from him?"

"No. I wouldn't waste much time on him. He's just another harmless transient. Let's go back to the office and see what the others came up with," Sam said as he started up the unmarked police car.

Three months elapsed since the bank heist. The countless of man hours spent on the case, led nowhere. Unfortunately, the only piece of evidence didn't reveal anything. Mickey and his team spent several additional man hours interviewing the bank employees and revisiting the sites of interest several times. It was a cold case. All the personnel involved in the investigation were eventually reassigned to other cases.

The bank robbery file eventually ended up on the 'unsolved' stack and Sam and his men went back to their routine of patrolling and protecting the City of Ventura.

◻ ◻ ◻

"Hey! Who are you? Whatcha doing looking into my tent?" the scruffy man demanded to know.

"Oh, I'm sorry. I was just trying to see if it was abandoned. I'm Gary and I'm searching for a spot to set up my shelter. I thought if this tent was abandoned, I would be able to use it. I mean no harm."

"It's not abandoned. It's mine. I may not stay in it every night, but everyone knows it's mine."

"Okay. Okay. I'll just keep looking," Gary told the stranger.

The man was holding his arm and grimaced in pain, as he bent over to enter the small tent.

"Are you all right?" Gary asked.

"I'm okay. Slipped down the boulders and hit my elbow when I jumped outta the boxcar. What's it to you, anyway?"

"I can look at it, if you wish. I used to be a medic in the Marines," Gary offered. The man reluctantly rolled up his sleeve and let Gary examine it. "Looks like a bad bruise. Don't appear to be broken. I have some extra aspirin. It'll help with the pain. Want some?"

"I guess, Doc. The skeptic kept a close eye on Gary's every move. I'm a veteran too, Korean Conflict. I have to watch my stuff, you know, so it doesn't get stolen."

"I understand. Look friend, you don't mind if I set up my shelter over there?" Gary asked, pointing a few yards down the sandy path."

"Last I heard, it was a free country," the senior resident said as he crouched into his tent.

That evening Gary received his first guest. "Hey Doc! Hope I didn't sound mean or rude earlier. I'm Todd. Wanna let you know, I appreciate you lookin' at my arm. "Gonna sit on the beach over there and watch the sunset. Gonna enjoy this bottle of liquid happiness. Wanna join me. It's my payment fer your doctoring."

"Sure. I could use a drink. And please, call me Gary. Haven't been a medic since I was in the military. How's that arm, Todd?"

That night, two hobos bonded over a bottle of cheap wine and some old war stories.

Gary and Todd hit it off quite well. If either one was not at camp, the other would watch out for the other's possessions. "It's called a symbiotic relationship," Gary tried explaining, "I take care of your stuff and you in turn watch mine. Together we live in harmony and serve each other. Like fish that help keep a shark's or whale's skin free of parasites. Todd, you understand?"

"If you're trying say that we help each other out? Just say it. You don't have to get all technical about it," Todd told his friend, as they both found humor in their social status.

At any given time, several transients' shelters could be found scattered throughout Hobo Jungle. Every once in a while mischievous pranksters rummaged through their belongings. But for the most part the vagabonds' sites were left untouched.

One afternoon, a man in a suit was snooping around Todd's camp. "Can I help you?" Gary asked as he approached the man.

"I'm just looking for an old friend. Appears he's not here. I'll come back later," the visitor replied as he turned and left.

The next day, Gary saw Todd speaking with the guy that was snooping around the campsite the day before. The man was surf fishing and gave Todd the fish he had caught.

"That guy was here yesterday. He was looking for you and said he would return. Guess he caught up with you," Gary said, as he helped clean and cook the fish.

"That's my brother. He works fer the city and comes around to make sure I'm doing okay. He helped me set up camp here, as a matter of fact he insisted on me putting my tent on this very spot. He said not to move it because it's the best location in the jungle," Todd shared.

"I'm the black sheep of the family. Never cared much fer a structured lifestyle. I enjoy this life. I don't have to answer to anyone and I'm not tied down to anyone or anything. In return, I have no stress and I have no bills," Todd proudly boasted.

"Ditto to everything you just said. Can you imagine us in a coat and tie?" Gary said laughing.

◘ ◘ ◘

In the following weeks Gary and Todd developed a sound and genuine friendship. "You treat me nicer than my brother does," Todd let Gary know. "I never had a close friend. I think maybe you might be my first best friend."

"Thanks Todd. Your friendship means a lot to me too."

Gary had seen and heard, first hand, the way Todd was treated by his brother. Todd was a slow learner and never finished school. He was drafted by the US Army and served two years before being discharged.

"After serving in the military I ended up drifting from town to town. I eventually returned to Ventura. This is my hometown you know. I guess this is where I belong," Todd told his hobo friend.

Todd's brother, a manipulator and control freak, used his brother to run errands and maintain his landscaped yard. Todd's compensation was usually in the form of chump change, a small bag of groceries, or a cheap bottle of wine.

One day, after being gone for two days, Gary returned to find a couple of young men pushing an inebriated Todd around. The drunken hobo's meager possessions were strewn throughout his campsite.

Enraged by the hoodlums, Gary charged toward the young men. He punched one squarely in the face and grabbed the other one's arm, tossing him a couple of feet through the air. Yanking the bloodied nosed man by the shirt, he got right up to his face and looked straight into his eyes, "If I ever see you two around here again, I'll break your bones. Now, get out of here."

Losing their traction on the dry sandy floor of the Jungle, the duo stumbled in their haste to escape Gary's wrath.

Turning his attention towards his friend, Gary promised him, "That's the last we'll see of those two punks. Are you okay Todd?"

"I'm okay. You sure did take care of them," he slurred. "You sure are a good fighter. Thanks Gary."

"It was nothing amigo. Just something I learned in the Marines. Glad you're fine."

The following day, Todd's brother approached Gary, "My brother says you saved his life. Says you're always there to help him. Tell me Gary, what is it you want from Todd? He doesn't have anything of value. He's just a hobo like you."

Caught off guard with this line of questioning, Gary replied, "I don't want anything of Todd's. I watch his camp and he watches mine. As a matter of fact I was just leaving. I'm hopping on a ride to Oxnard. I'll be gone two nights. Todd said he'll watch my stuff. We're just two veterans watching out for each other."

"Okay Gary. Listen, I just don't want to see anyone taking advantage of my brother. But you've been good to him. If you ever need anything, you just let Todd know. I'll help if I can."

❏ ❏ ❏

"Why are you digging in my tent", Todd demanded to know. You're throwing dirt and sand on everything."

"Keep quiet you fool. I'm just looking for something," his brother told him."

"Whatcha lookin' fer?" You're digging where I sleep," the puzzled man told him, starting to get agitated."

"Shut up and go keep watch", Todd was ordered, receiving a sharp slap across the back of his head.

The silhouette formed by an old oil lamp reflected a man's image, inside the tent, pulling something out of the ground. He emerged out of the tent wiping off a dirty brown case. "Don't just stand there, you idiot, bring me my lamp."

Handing his brother the oil lamp, Todd inquired, "What is that? How did you know it was there?"

"Todd, this is only some old stuff from my college days. I just remembered where me and my college buddies buried it," his brother told him.

Within seconds Todd and his brother were surrounded by several men. "FBI," they announced. "Put the suitcase down and place the lamp on the ground. Both of you slowly put your hands on top of your head. Now kneel down on the ground."

The brown leather case contained the stolen money, the robber's costume, makeup, a fake nose, a wig, glasses, and a hat. Both men were read their Miranda Rights and transported to the local FBI Branch Office, where they were interrogated.

Todd was released that night and driven back to Hobo Jungle.

"Who's going to take care of my brother?"

"Maybe you should have thought about his welfare before robbing that bank," Agent Cruz told the robbery suspect.

"But to put you mind at ease, Todd will be offered a chance to enroll in a federally funded program geared towards helping homeless veterans get jobs, an education, and housing. You can thank Gary for that."

"You mean Gary, that bum at 'Hobo Jungle'? What can he ever do to help anyone? the suspect asked.

"Yeah, that's him. Oh, and by the way, Gary is one of my best undercover agents," Agent Cruz explained. His clever disguise and patience paid off. It was his patience and good police work that helped crack this case. Clever how you placed Todd's tent over your buried treasure."

"What, he tipped you off?"

"No. I interviewed an old man who told me he had seen a stranger with what resembled the brown suitcase in the picture I showed him. Later, from a distance, he saw someone get up after the train passed over him. The man walked off the bridge limping, and climbed into a big shiny white car. Based on that information, I directed ten undercover agents to set up camp sites throughout Hobo Jungle."

"But you really want to know who and what first tipped me off? You did . . . you and the heavy rains. The rains created mudslides which completely washed away the road and paths to the beach the night prior to the bank heist. The area was inaccessible and off limits. So you see Sam . . . you couldn't have been fishing at 'the Rincon' the day the bank was robbed."

LITTLE LADY

*When children don't listen to parents,
and their slates they fill with events,
that might alter their health, or at risk put their lives
for not listening, to what their parents meant.*

—R. Quero

Little Lady

"Hello my Little Lady," teased dad, "Where have you been all morning?"

"Why do you always call me Little Lady?" Peaches asked. "You know I like to be called by my real name."

"I know Peaches, your Mom insisted on naming you. I thought Camellia or Rose would have been nice. But she said that all her sisters were named after flowers and she wanted something unique. To be quite honest, I think Peaches is a pretty name. However, you'll always be my Little Lady."

He proceeded to explain, "You see, little girls are 'daddy's little girls', especially the first female. You're the spitting image of your Mom; she's my Lady, which makes you my Little Lady. Now, would you rather I call you my Little Girl?"

"No Dad, I guess as long as Mom still calls me Peaches, you can call me Little Lady."

"Peaches, every time you try to evade your father's questions you always play this name game of yours. Now answer your father," said Mom with a stern voice.

"I was playing in the flower field Dad. It's such a beautiful, sunny day. All the kids were out there."

"You know how Dad worries about you," said her Mom. "It's pretty close to the time that plane comes over the fields and sprays that insecticide. The pilots don't care who or what is down there. Their job is to spray the crop before the flowers are cut and sent to market."

"That's right Little Lady and the chemicals they use now-a-days are still quite potent. I don't care what the FDA, or what those other health organizations say. The truth is that one can get cancer or even die from exposure to those sprays," her Dad warned.

"Yeah, I know," said Little Lady, rolling her eyes and trying not to let Dad catch her in the act. "But what I was going to tell you . . ."

He smiled and immediately interrupted her, "Don't roll those little black eyes at me. I'm serious about my take on the use of chemicals. And don't tell me that I'm paranoid about the whole notion. Just look around and listen to what's being said. It's all bad for the environment."

"I know Dad. But what I was going to say is that there's some honeysuckle growing on the other side of the flower field. You can suck the sweet honey from the flower. The darker yellow flowers are the sweetest; their leaves are covered with aphids, so I guess the fields have not been sprayed, yet."

"Oh, Little Lady, you see, that's what I'm talking about. You're still too young to be able to tell the difference if they sprayed or not. Some varieties of aphids are resistant to certain chemicals. You took the risk of getting sick or maybe dying. I just don't trust those chemicals."

"Gosh dad, you always make it sound like the end of the world is near. I understand your concern and I appreciate you watching out for me, but I'm pretty careful. I'm not a little baby anymore," she protested.

"You're right. I guess at some point I have to learn to let go. But that doesn't mean I don't love you. Tomorrow is your first flight alone to your grandparents for the 4th of July weekend. You may not be a little baby, but you're still not quite an adult yet. It'll be a good test for both of us. I'll try not to be worried sick, but I also know that you are capable of taking care of yourself."

◦ ◦ ◦

Peaches had a wonderful time visiting with her grandparents. They lived along the riverbanks of the Mighty Mississippi River. Every day she spent hours watching the riverboats and barges. *Goodness, what a busy river. I wonder where all those people are going?* she thought to herself, *I'll have to ask Granddad.*

"Granddad, where are all these boats and people going?" she asked, knowing that she would get a nice, long, interesting story.

"Well, sweetie, some of those folks are on vacation and are just taking a boat ride. Some of those ships are carrying food, merchandise, or supplies. They're destined for a market place, somewhere down the river, maybe as far as New Orleans. And that barge you see, that's sitting low in the water, is probably carrying coal, wheat, or some other commodity. It's all going to market or maybe to a power plant. Some of what they're transporting will go to a packaging plant or to a storage silo. They use large cranes and conveyer belts to unload the merchandise. Now, Peaches, I don't mean to sound like an alarmist, but you need to be careful because its mosquito season and the trucks come by spraying that smelly chemical fog."

"Granddad, you and Dad sound alike. You two are always worrying about DDT, FDA, CDC, and BUG sprays," laughed Peaches.

"We love you Peaches," Grandma reminded her, "that's why we worry."

"I know, I love you too," Peaches told her grandparents.

The weekend spent with her grandparents was full of fun and interesting things they had planned for her. A trip to the zoo afforded Peaches a chance to be right up close to animals she had never seen. At the park they spent time enjoying the many varieties of flowers. They also watched people play softball or walking their dogs.

"This is really neat," Peaches kept telling her grandparents, "it's the most fun I have ever had."

They spent one morning riding the trolley and looking at all the large beautiful homes along the route. That afternoon they came across an open carriage, used to give tours through the old part of town. It was drawn by a large white horse. The same thought ran through all three of their minds.

"It was a great idea to hitch a ride," Grandma said, "and just think, this horse drawn carriage passes right in front of our home."

The grand finale, on this short vacation, was the Fourth of July fireworks. Peaches had already fallen asleep, but her grandparents woke her up to experience the event. They were able to view the colorful display from her grandparent's home.

"Oh, how pretty," exclaimed Peaches with excitement, every time a firework lit the night sky.

Each firework just kept getting bigger, louder, and more spectacular. The finale was multiple explosions of colors that seemed to go on forever.

"What did you think about that, Peaches?" Grandpa asked.

There was no response. Peaches had fallen asleep.

The next morning the three had breakfast together. "Don't eat too much, Peaches," Grandma warned, "you don't want to feel sick on your flight home."

"We love you very much," they told her as she prepared to leave.

"I know. I love you too."

It saddened Peaches to know that her grandparents were getting older and that this might be the last time she would see them. Her parents never mentioned it, but she knew that this was the main reason they had insisted she make the visit.

The flight home was uneventful. It was a little breezy at the higher elevations. Otherwise, the weather was perfect for flying. Unlike the headwinds, which slowed the flight en route to her grandparents, the tailwinds helped make the flight much shorter on the return trip.

□ □ □

"Dad, while on vacation I watched some boys fishing. They used earth worms and crickets for bait. I felt sorry for those worms and crickets. Why couldn't they just use fake lures?"

"Some fish are attracted to the real thing and are not easily fooled. They know what they eat every day and can identify it as real or as a man-made lure. You see Little Lady; in the animal kingdom just about everything is part of the food chain. The fish naturally eat worms, crickets, mosquitoes, and other insects. Crickets eat bugs. Lizards eat bugs and bugs eat other bugs, like aphids. Snakes eat lizards and rodents. And of course people eat fish and some animals too. Everything in the food chain is recognized as such. But there are also some that would attempt to eat something that is not food, like a fish going after a lure. Does that clear things up for you?"

"Ah, I guess. But dad, aren't some people and certain animals or insects vegetarians?"

"Yes they are. And that brings up another good point. If vegetables and other plant foods are not washed properly, you can get sick. Some people even die from e-coli or the chemicals used on plants."

"There you go again, Dad. I think it's time for me to go play. See you later."

After spending the afternoon playing in the backyard garden, Peaches rushed in to tell her parents what she had seen. "I saw a lizard with eyes that moved in opposite directions. It was looking up in one direction with one eye and towards the back with the other eye. It was really weird," Peaches excitedly shared.

"I'm afraid of lizards," her mother said. "I'd keep away from them if I were you."

"I know Mom. I kept a good distance from it. But this one was so colorful, it caught my attention. I watched it for quite a while. It moved at a snail's pace and when it saw a fly, at lightning speed, it snatched it with its tongue. It had a really long tongue. You should've seen it. I think it might've been at least twice as long as it's body."

"Sounds like you saw a chameleon," Dad pitched in. "They look like miniature versions of dinosaurs and are quite an intriguing work of nature. If you're a bug they can ruin your day. It's all part of that food chain we were talking about. Listen Little Lady, I heard the gardener say that he will be spraying the garden tomorrow. So play somewhere else so that you don't get any of that stinky stuff on you. Maybe a good rain will come and wash all that poison away."

"Okay Dad, if you say so," Peaches said rolling her eyes. "Mom, I'm going out to watch the chameleon."

"Keep your distance Peaches. I just don't trust snakes and lizards."

"I will Mom."

Good grief, I know they mean well, but I think I can take care of myself in our own back yard, Peaches thought as she returned to the garden.

Once out in the garden, Little Lady had to search long and hard to locate the chameleon. It had moved to a different area of the garden and changed its color to camouflage itself.

I can't believe I'm actually looking for this lizard, Little Lady found amusement in her thoughts.

She enthusiastically watched as the lizard methodically moved its eyes, independent one from the other and in opposite directions, seeking out its next gourmet meal.

Maybe if I sneak up on it, quietly and slowly, it won't run away, Little Lady planned a much closer approach to the reptile.

When she was certain the miniature dinosaur had both eyes focused away from her, she inched a wee bit closer. From the thrill and excitement of her backyard excursion, she could feel her heart pounding hard and fast.

Now I know what it must feel like to be a big game hunter on his first safari, she thought.

Suddenly, with lightning speed and accuracy, the chameleon's long tongue reached out and snatched the "Little Lady" bug.

KATIE

> **W**hen you meet someone you care for,
> get their full name, their number, and then more.
> It'll be useful for you, when you begin to explore
> the company you think they still work for.
>
> —*R. Quero*

Katie

From the back of the transport plane the jumpmaster recorded Chris's jump. In the log, under May 13, 2001 he entered Christopher Logan's name and in the "Jump #" column he penned in "100". In the Altitude column he wrote "3500f". "Okay, they're all out, we're clear to return to the airport," he told the pilot over the intercom.

Christopher, a successful actor, was part of a small breed of actors that insisted on doing their own stunts.

◘ ◘ ◘

The day before the jump shot, Chris argued his case with the producers. "There's no reason why we have to pay a stuntman to jump, when I am qualified to do the scene myself. Not only will it be my 100th jump, but it can serve as good publicity for the movie. Besides, I have jumped over every state in the Union except for Louisiana. I need this one under my belt," he pleaded.

"You got your way with the producers Chris," the director later told him, "now let's see if we can get this shot on the first take. I have two cameramen jumping with you. I also have three more on the ground shooting the jump from different angles."

◽ ◽ ◽

Christopher felt his heart pounding extremely fast, as he scanned the countryside outside of the Baton Rouge city limits. But then again, that was the sensation he always experienced after leaping from an aircraft. The free fall was uneventful but exhilarating, nonetheless.

"This is what it's all about," he spoke into the microphone in his helmet. The two cameramen that had also jumped gave him thumbs up.

"Boys will be boys," the director said, watching and listening from the landing site.

The cold air rushing and pressing against his face at 125 mph forced his cheeks to spread, forming an animated smile. But deep inside Christopher was grinning, ear-to-ear, with the greatest feeling of content for accomplishing two of his long sought goals: his triple digit jump and the fiftieth US State was on the record.

What a sensational feeling, he thought. *Aside from the cameramen, it's just me, God, the beautiful clear blue sky, and the lush green planet below.*

Except for the muffled sound of rushing air, everything was calm and quiet.

Vehicles on the ground were now the size of large toy trucks. It was time to activate the parachute. He pulled on the ripcord once . . . twice . . . and then the third time. The main chute wasn't deploying and the reserve chute wouldn't open either. Trying frantically to manually extract the parachute proved futile. The ground was rapidly approaching. With hardly enough time to whisper a prayer, he closed his eyes tightly and waited for the inevitable impact with earth.

The loud buzzer from the alarm clock startled Christopher out of his nightmare. He was completely soaked from head to toe with perspiration. It seemed that at least once a week he relived that terrible accident. After months of therapy with a psychologist he was still unable to shake these recurring nightmares.

◽ ◽ ◽

"Chris, three years have passed since that day in May," his brother Quincy, mentioned over dinner. "It's a miracle you even survived the impact. You spent one month on a mechanical ventilator followed by an additional two months before being transferred from intensive care to a regular hospital room. Later you endured months of sweat and pain in physical rehabilitation. Your recovery was remarkable, considering the injuries you sustained. Almost very bone in your body was broken or crushed, including multiple facial bones that were shattered. I can understand why you have those nightmares."

"I suppose I am being impatient, Quincy. The doctors say that with time, the dreams might subside. But it's also the terrible headaches. They're practically unbearable."

"You had some cranial trauma and although your skull remained intact a small drainage tube needed to be inserted into the skull. It helped relieve the pressure from the swelling. I've always said you had a hard head," teased his brother. "I think that's what saved your life."

Since the accident, Christopher had regained ninety percent mobility on his dominant side and almost eighty percent of the other side. He walked with a cane to support the weaker side and the prognosis at this point was that this was probably the extent of his physical recovery. Permanent rods, pins, and plates pretty much kept a good portion of his skeletal frame in place.

"The road to recovery has been long and slow. I strongly believe that my bouts with depression played a role in my slow recovery. But, I think the depression is finally starting to slowly vanish. Anyway, I'm not experiencing much of it."

"Brother, I can tell the difference. You socialize more and you have been spending the past couple of years more involved with your work," Quincy told him. You're a born fighter and along with all the moral support from your friends and family, you have come a long, long way."

"You're right Quincy. And I have to give credit to the doctors, nurses, and therapists that spent so much time encouraging and working with me."

"You mean like Katie? Haven't heard you mention her since you were discharged from the hospital," Quincy asked, trying to get his brother to open up.

"There's a lot I need to work out before I decide to make my life more complicated," Chris said.

Quincy took this as a signal to drop the subject about Katie and immediately changed the subject.

"Chris, remember when dad used to take us to the movie studios and we would spend a good portion of the day playing in the vast acres of movie sets"?

"Yeah, we didn't know he was an electrical engineer. We thought he was a movie star."

"I don't know who he knew at Hollywood Movie Studios, but we were allowed to attend school in makeshift class rooms with all those snobbish child stars."

"Gosh Quincy, those were fun times. I knew then and there that I wanted to be an actor."

"And I knew that I wanted to write for the big screen. Who would've thought that both of our dreams would come true?"

"Dad knew," Chris blurted out, after a few seconds of silence. "He always used to tell us to follow our dreams and we would be happy in life."

Heeding his father's advice, Chris started trying out for small parts in television commercials and then as an extra in movies. As a young teenager, he landed minor roles in movies geared toward the younger generation.

His big break came at the age of eighteen, when he played in a supporting role opposite one of America's big screen sweethearts. This led to a leading role as a young detective transported back in time. His character was able to solve crimes and mysteries using unorthodox investigative techniques. The role launched him into the world of "movie stardom" and earned him his first major cinema award.

◻ ◻ ◻

During Christopher's hospitalization, Quincy flew from Los Angeles to Baton Rouge once a week and would stay a couple of days at Chris's bedside before returning back to his job in California.

On one occasion, when Chris woke up, he saw Quincy working on his laptop.

"Still working on that movie script"? "Have you seen Katie? I thought I heard her voice."

"No, Chris. It might've been Nurse Vera. She was here a few minutes ago."

Quincy had not met Katie, but felt like he knew her from all that Christopher had said about her. She obviously worked night shifts and opposite days than when he was there. He was more than eager to meet this special person his brother had taken a liking to. Every other sentence was "Katie this. Katie that."

▫ ▫ ▫

Christopher had always felt just as comfortable writing, directing, or looking through the camera lens as he did acting. His knowledge, drive, and love for the movie industry helped open doors; giving him the opportunity to continue his illustrious career with films after his near fatal accident. This was where he now found himself, still contributing and still as successful in his movie making efforts as when he played the lead roles.

"Returning to work proved to be just as important to the strengthening of my psychological wellbeing, as physical therapy was to regaining the mobility and strength of my body. Movies are my life and I love everything about this profession," he mentioned at an awards banquet.

After several awards for his writings and directing, he started thinking about his next project. *Maybe Quincy has been right all along. Writing a story or script based on my hospital experience might help get things off my chest and at the same time serve as a form of therapy.*

"The more I think about those painful months of struggling to survive and learning how to use my body again . . . the more I appreciate the patience and care rendered by the medical staff," he shared with Quincy. "Those folks," he proclaimed, "will be the basis for my next movie script."

His friends, his business associates, and his brother all commented on his up-lifted spirits whenever he mentioned Nurse Katie's name. He regretted he had not kept in touch with her. Persistent encouragement and prodding from his inner circle of friends (and Quincy), helped him decide to look her up. That is, under the pretense of research for his writings . . . of course.

He thought back to the first time he saw Nurse Katie's face. He sat at the computer and typed as his mind drifted back in time. *I don't remember much of what was going on when I first started coming out of the drug induced coma. I vaguely recall lying in a bed, unable to move, with a tube going into my mouth that was pushing air into my lungs. Later I learned that I was hooked up to a ventilator, which helped me to breathe. I also seem to remember, that*

I was completely naked and someone was wiping my body with a cool wet washcloth. The dampness evaporated into the cool ambient air and I could feel a cold chill come over my entire body. I started to shiver uncontrollably.

"You'll be all right Mr. Logan," a soft sweet gentle voice assured me. "I'm just finishing your morning bath. My name is Katie. I'm your nurse and I'll be taking care of you," she said as she pulled a sheet over my body. I tried to focus in on the caregiver but gradually drifted back into a deep sleep. It seemed as if every time I woke up Katie was there.

Throughout the weeks of his recovery, he and Katie spent a lot of time talking and getting to know each other. She played an important role in his recuperation both as a health care provider and as a friend. She was a great source of encouragement and he cherished the days she was there. Room 318, in the ICU, had become a little heaven on earth when she was there with him.

After he was transferred out of the ICU, to a regular hospital room, Katie visited with him on a regular basis. She was also there for him when he was transferred to the in-patient rehabilitation center. Katie would always visit in the evening prior to starting her night shift, staying there until he fell asleep.

On one of her visits, Katie took pictures of the both of them together. "You'll need a picture for your scrapbook to remind you of your days in the hospital," she told him.

She was careful not to compromise her professional standing with him and he was just as cautious not to put her in a position that might jeopardize her job.

However, the more time they spent together, the more the unspoken affection for each other grew. They established a unique and caring relationship that would last through eternity. He affectionately nicknamed her "K", and she, in-turn, went from Mr. Logan, to Christopher, to Chris. Whatever name she called him, it was always with a twinkle in her eyes.

Upon discharge from the rehabilitation center Christopher lost touch with "K". His life with his friends and his professional obligations kept him fully occupied. He devoted himself entirely to his career. Although the fast pace of Hollywood was therapeutic, it also contributed to his unconscious suppression of his feelings for "K".

▫ ▫ ▫

Over three years has passed since I last saw Katie, now here I am waiting on a flight to Louisiana, Christopher thought, as he killed time strolling through the corridors of the Los Angeles International Airport. The flight had been delayed due to heavy fog in the area, which meant that departure from California would be late at night.

After landing in Baton Rouge, Louisiana, he went directly to the hotel, checked in, and slept soundly until 7:30 A.M.

That morning, he had a hearty breakfast in the hotel restaurant and then took a cab to the hospital. He found himself moving along at a more than normal pace as he made his way down the long hallway leading to the ICU.

He was arriving unannounced and prayed that during the past three years Katie had not gotten romantically involved with someone else. Now more than ever he wished he had kept in touch with her or that he had at least made a call letting her know he would be in town.

His mind was bombarded with many questions. *Will she be glad to see me? Does she have any romantic feelings for me? What if she has moved on with her life and I'm not even in the picture? Why should she have waited for me when I didn't even make an attempt to contact her?*

He began to doubt the validity of his visit and started to feel foolish about this quest of his. *Maybe I'm pursuing a relationship that never really existed. Maybe, the feelings were not mutual and she was just doing her duties as a nurse. It doesn't matter,* he thought, *I'm here now and I'm going to follow through with what I came to do.*

"If it's meant to be . . . it's meant to be," he found himself saying out loud, as he reached the ICU.

Turning the corner he looked up and saw on the open door, "ICU 318". His heart sped up a little. Looking into the dimly lit room, he saw that there wasn't a patient assigned to the room. The smell of the clean, fresh antiseptic cleaning solution brought back a flood of mixed emotions associated with his stay in the hospital.

"Can I help you sir?" he heard a lady's voice ask.

Sitting in the far corner of the room, he saw a young nurse in blue scrubs working on her charts.

He stated his business and asked if she knew a nurse named Katie. She told him that she was fairly new, but that the Charge Nurse might be able to help him.

Maggie, the Charge Nurse, wasn't of much help either, but gave him a good lead, "We don't currently have a Katie on staff and I didn't know any of the staff that was here when you were a patient. You see Mr. Logan, since your hospitalization, a national conglomerate purchased the hospital and the entire staff was replaced. But I do know that Bea's Medical Staffing (BMS), an agency that handles medical staffing augmentation, used to provide nurses to this hospital."

"How can I get in contact with this agency?" Chris wanted to know.

"Oh, that's easy," Maggie said. "They're located across the street from the main entrance to the hospital's emergency room. I know Bea quite well. I'll give her a call and let her know that you'll be going her way."

Ms. Bea was waiting at the front door of the corporate office complex. "Mr. Logan, the ICU called and said you would be swinging by here. You didn't have to walk across, I could have sent a car to pick you up," she told him, noticing the walking cane.

"Thanks Ms. Bea but walking is good therapy. Hey! I think I know you," he added searching his memory bank. "Yeah, I remember now. You made the 'Top Ten Female Entrepreneurs' list for this year. Congratulations. And please, call me Chris."

"Chris, you may call me Bea. I'm delighted to meet you. I'm a big fan of yours. I've kept up with all those awards you have been honored with. I should be the one giving out congratulations. Anyway, Maggie said you needed help finding a friend that worked as a nurse when you were a patient. Let's go up to my office and see what we can come up with."

Christopher filled Bea in on his stay at the hospital and meeting his friend Katie. "Unfortunately, I didn't have the sense, to ask Katie her last name."

"Chris," Bea said, "Katie is a pretty common name. We must have at least 200-300 Katies in our data bank spelled all kinds of ways. But as you must know, there are strict rules about giving out information on our employees. One good thing is that there is a copy of every employee's picture on file. It's a copy of the one used on our BMS ID card. If you can identify her face, I can attempt contact with Katie and let her know that you want to get in touch with her. That's the best I can do without breaching the employee's confidentiality. Anyway, it's all in the computer so it'll be a little easier to search for this Katie of yours."

Nearly four hours of viewing photo shots on the computer proved to be futile. Christopher was exhausted, disillusioned, and about to give up. Bea suggested that he take a lunch break and if he had the time she had some inactive files he could go through after lunch. "Maybe Katie is tucked away in one of those files," she mentioned, giving him a glimmer of hope.

Following a scrumptious Cajun lunch buffet, Christopher returned to his hotel to retrieve an out-of-focus snap shot of Katie, the only picture he had of her. Upon returning to Bea's office he found her with six large boxes of files for him to look through. He handed her the copy of Katie's picture.

"This photo is pretty blurry, but she kind of reminds me of Katherine Powers, my very best friend. But she died after a lengthy battle with cancer. I spent the night in her room when she passed away. I'll never forget that night, May 12, 2001. It was 8 P.M. She was in Room 318, overlooking the river."

"What a coincidence, my accident was Friday the 13th, and I occupied that same room the following evening," Chris told Bea.

"Then I'm sure my Katherine isn't your Katie. Besides I don't have her photo. Even though she was a nurse, she didn't work for BMS".

After going through half of the extra files Bea had taken out of storage for him to search through, Chris finally decided to call it a day. "I'm tired and my neck is getting stiff from going through all these files," a frustrated Chris told Bea. "Do you suppose I can come back tomorrow and continue my search?"

"Chris, you may come by any time tomorrow. You can work out of the small conference room across from my office. You've met my secretary, if I'm not here, she'll assist you if you need help," Bea offered as they walked to the elevators.

Once outside Bea's Medical Staffing, Chris saw a parked taxi across the street. His mind was completely preoccupied with his failure to locate Katie on his first day in Baton Rouge. He had come all this way thinking that it would be a simple and fast reunion. Dodging passing cars, he made his way across the street, to the parked cab.

He was about to get into the cab when, without warning and out of nowhere, a car came barreling, out of control, directly towards him. He was hit hard, hurling him through the air. Ironically, he landed a few steps from the entrance to the emergency room. The injuries were critical and he was immediately taken to surgery. After three long hours in surgery, he was transferred to the ICU.

He was drifting in and out of consciousness but could faintly hear the PA announcement, "CODE BLUE ICU 318. CODE BLUE ICU 318". A medical team had assembled around him and he could hear them discussing their options. The alarms in the background were loud and annoying but he was able to hear the doctors, "We're losing him, there's not much we can do. We did what we could in surgery but he has extensive internal injuries. Chest compressions will only traumatize the heart even more."

Christopher couldn't speak. He had a tube down his throat. Somehow, he knew it was time. His mind and body felt as light as a feather. As if he had crossed the threshold into a state of euphoria. *Maybe it's the morphine. It doesn't matter. It's a calm and peaceful feeling,* he thought.

Then the shrill of the heart monitor's flat line alarm pierced the air. In a far distance, he heard the doctor pronouncing him. "He's gone. Stop all resuscitative efforts. Time 20:00", the physician in-charge of the "code" professionally and respectfully announced.

At the very split second the doctor started making his statement, Christopher felt a cool sensation envelope his entire body, as if he were being bathed. He felt a warm hand on his then a soft, sweet gentle voice said, "Chris, it's me Katie. I'll be taking care of you."

BORN TO DANCE

***If** dancing is all that you know,*
then express it . . . just make it a show.
Take a few months to practice,
come out and present it,
and who knows? . . . It might be a hit.

—*R. Quero*

Born to Dance

The staff was hurriedly trying to wipe me dry following the grand finale. The spotlight was hot and bright, and the flashes from the cameras made me squint even harder. Standing room only I heard someone announce. I was caught up with emotion. One couldn't ask for more on the day of his debut. I bawled like a baby.

"He's our son . . . the dancer," I heard my mother proudly say.

Well yeah, I thought. *Is there anything else in life?*

I don't want to sound arrogant, snobbish, or even disrespectful toward other professions or favorite past times, but I think dancing should be everyone's first love.

By the way, I'm Randy. Please let me explain why I feel this way. To do so, you must come with me down memory lane . . . my memory lane. Then maybe you'll get a better understanding of why dancing is the love of my life.

You see, as far back as I can remember music and moving to music has always been part of my life. At various award ceremonies, in their acceptance speeches, recipients give thanks to their mothers for helping them fulfill their dreams. So, at this point, I feel like I too must acknowledge, and with deepest gratitude, thank my mom and dad for being there and introducing me to a myriad of styles when it comes to music.

My mom enjoys every conceivable genre as it relates to music. Be it gospel, blues, classical, or just plain old rock and roll. She listens to rap, new wave, and country. Music fills the house from the moment she wakes up to the minute she goes to bed at night. Even then, music softly plays in the background. Sometimes, late at night, I would hear the radio playing some of Glenn Miller's swing, Frank Sinatra's swooning, or Scott Joplin's ragtime. She often moves her feet to the music while she sleeps. "I have restless leg syndrome," she keeps reminding dad.

"Yeah, sure Honey," Dad humors her. He knows better than to argue the point.

She even listens to music in foreign languages. In a Chinese restaurant she once hushed its patrons so that she could listen to the music in the background. That was the first and only time I heard Dad say anything harsh to Mom.

Both my parents love Latin music. They compete professionally and excel in salsa, tango, and bolero competitions. Maybe that's why I especially enjoy the Latin rhythms. Anyway, I'll share more about their professional career later.

"Drama, pure drama," Dad always teases mom when she listens to opera. Although she doesn't understand a word of Italian, she always cries her eyes out when she hears various movements or songs from an opera.

"I can't help it", she says, "it just touches my heart very deep."

I must have inherited that trait from her. There's just something about opera that makes me want to stretch out my arms, as if exaggerating the movements of the actors on stage.

"You're feeling it, aren't you Randy?" Mom always asked.

Truth be known, Dad's reaction to opera isn't much better. Yes, he teases Mom, but when it comes to opera he too gets emotional. I remember, on several occasions, when both of them were in the parlor listening to some tenor hitting those high notes and my parents reaching out for each other's hands. Both crying like babies.

Personally, I think my parents are so emotionally sensitive that they can feel the music in their inner most being and simply react accordingly.

Yup, I got that from them too.

But oh, how I love the old time music. Give me that jitterbug or a good swing tune anytime of the day or night. As with Mom, when it's playing, I feel good inside. That music makes me want to dance.

"That's it Randy. Just let the music move you," I was encouraged.

I learned, at an early age in life, how to use my arms and legs to express myself through dancing. I might not have looked graceful or even professional at times, but it sure felt good to me.

It was the same thing with swimming. The sensation of just floating there, suspended in place by the surrounding water. I guess that's the closest I'll ever come to knowing what it's like to float in space. I think water and music go along wonderfully. Although it's not my forte, I have come to enjoy practicing my own aquatic and acrobatic skills to soft music in the background. For me it all ties in together. Music and dancing go hand-in-hand and I just happen to believe that it's part of my very being.

Are you beginning to understand where I'm coming from? Am I making any sense? Please hang in there. I'll try to make it clearer.

I mentioned that Mom and Dad were professional dancers. It all started when they were small kids. At the age of six or seven, both were enrolled, by their parents, in the same dance school. At the age of eleven they were teamed up for competition. It didn't take long for the dance instructors, the parents, and the kids to realize because of their size, talent, and love for dancing that the two made a formidable dance couple. That's was nearly twenty eight years ago and they've been dancing together ever since. Well, that is until a few months ago when Mom starting getting sick. We'll talk more about that later.

Did I tell you that they own a small dance studio? They teach ballroom dancing, jazz, and line dancing. They specialize in Latin dances and the classic ballroom waltzes. They are good. And I don't just say that because they're my parents, but they have competed and won several national and international awards.

You see, it's in the blood. I got my dancing genes from both of them. Blame them for my insatiable desire to move to the music.

One day, at the studio, while practicing a fast and complicated routine Mom fainted and twisted her ankle. She, gracefully of course, slid down unto the floor. Dad still had his arm around her, which helped to break the fall.

"I've got you Honey," he let her know.

When she came to, Dad told her, "You probably passed out from the long and fast series of spins. You seem all right, but your ankle is pretty swollen."

The doctor examined her foot and recommended she treat it with ice packs and an aspirin when the pain flared up. "Stay off it for at least a couple of weeks and see how it heals. By the way, from now on eat something before doing any strenuous workouts. Your health is more important than that slim figure of yours."

That seemed to be the start of her slow decline. "We'll have to put our competition on hold," Mom notified Dad, "Just until I start feeling stronger."

Shortly after that, her condition worsened and Mom had to cut back on giving private lessons. At this point she was only working an abbreviated schedule. When she showed up it was only for a short while. Mom is the choreographer for the studio's classes so she insisted on being at the studio. "I want to be there, at least to talk the class through their steps. I can call out corrections or encourage the students from the side of the room." Eventually, even this she relegated to her assistant.

Dad, concerned over the decline in Mom's health, called Grandma Stevens on the phone, "Her breathing has become more labored and she starting to lose her strength much faster by the day. She's also spending more time at home, in bed."

Grandma Stevens volunteered to move in, temporarily, to help care for Mom. On rare occasions, when Mom felt strong enough, she had Grandma drive her to the studio where she enjoyed the music and watched the dance routines.

"I think the stress and fear of learning how things might turn out has definitely affected her mental status. I've tried to comfort her and spend a few hours assuring and reassuring her that everything would be all right. She cries a lot. Sometimes for no apparent reason, she starts to uncontrollably weep," Dad explained Mom's condition to Doctor Jones.

The doctor said, "Its depression. Just let her know that she's not going through this alone. Try, also, to keep her calm. She needs rest," he told Dad and Grandma.

During this time I tried my best to behave and stay quiet. But as you all know, that's not easy for a growing boy.

"All of you are on vacation," Grandma Stevens announced. She did all the washing, cleaning, and cooking. "I'm here to take care of the mother, son, and the husband. "And furthermore, I don't care what the doctors say. One can't keep it quiet all day. Music stirs the soul and makes you feel good," she let her intentions be known.

She played music all day and Mom enjoyed it. Even in her sickest moments, when nausea overcame her, she wanted music in the background and Grandma obliged her. Sometimes Grandma would keep Mom entertained with her dancing. Well maybe it was the lack of dance skills that amused Mom, more than anything. You see, Grandma just doesn't have it. Anyway, Grandma is totally convinced that she can water the eyes of the judges in competition. She made Mom smile a lot during those months of discomfort and pain.

Dad always tried to ruffle her feathers, "You'll water their eyes, all right. But only because they'll be crying from laughing so hard."

Good thing Grandma has a good sense of humor. Otherwise, she would have gone home and left all the work for Dad.

It was about 2 A.M. and I woke up to Mom's screaming. "It hurts too much," she kept telling Dad. It bothered me that Mom was in so much pain, but there was nothing I could do about it. Sometimes, I reached out and gently touched her with my hands. But tonight was different. I could sense the urgency of the moment. I tried to close it all out, curled up in a fetal position, and prayed, *Please God, make her pain go away.*

"It'll be all right. We're here with you. Try to stay calm. Relax. I'm going to drive you to the hospital," Dad rattled off every calming line he could conjure up. I could tell from the fast cadence and the nervousness in his voice, that his anxiety level was elevated too.

"I called the hospital to let them know we were on our way," Grandma told Dad, as we rushed out the house and into the car.

Fortunately, there was hardly any traffic that time of the night. The majority of the traffic lights were blinking amber, so Dad didn't have very many red lights to contend with. I'm sure the pedal was to the metal as he navigated through the nearly deserted streets of the city.

Jumping the curb, he came to a screeching halt just inches from the main entrance. The front tire on the passenger's side of the vehicle activated the automatic door leading into the hospital.

Once admitted, the nurses and doctors started working on Mom.

"I need some vital signs, hook her up to the monitors," the doctor instructed the medical team. "Get me some labs STAT and have respiratory therapy start a breathing treatment."

"Let's change her into a hospital gown," the nurse told the aide.

The staff completed their assessments and gave their report to the doctor, "Aside from her admit diagnosis, she developed diabetes, her blood pressure is elevated, she's retaining fluids and is having difficulty catching her breath."

"Get some supplemental oxygen started and prep her for surgery." Dr. Jones told his intern.

I really didn't understand anything they were saying but it sounded like mom was pretty critical.

A few months ago the doctor recommended she voluntarily enter the hospital for rest and to be close at hand in case things took a turn for the worse. Mom, with her stubborn ways, opted to stay at home until the very last minute. I've always felt that it was a bad judgment call on Mom's part.

"We'll have to do emergency surgery," the doctor told the family.

The medical staff practically ran down the hall as they pushed the gurney with Mom on it. Dad and the Doctor Jones trailed the entourage. "We're taking her directly into the surgical suite," the doctor said, "There's not much time, we'll have to act swiftly."

He had just finished scrubbing up, when the nurse called out, "Doctor, we need you in here right away."

A caesarean section had to be performed. The ten and a half pound baby was breached and the umbilical cord was wrapped around his neck. Once out and separated from the cord, the baby took his first breath and pinked up fast.

The staff worked fast as they wiped me dry and then handed me to Dad, who carefully laid me on Mom's bosom.

"Look Honey", Mom said to Dad with pride, "Randy's moving his legs. He's our son . . . the dancer."

IN A WORLD OF SILENCE

*When your closest confidant is Mom,
and her hearing is gone, so you sign.
If her eyesight she loses, to her you still come,
No matter what happens in time.*

—R. Quero

In A World of Silence

"I hate always coming to you with my personal problems, but you're the only one that listens and understands." Although her mother's hearing was completely gone Debra always felt comfortable talking things out with her.

Margaret, Debra's mom, was mute. A severe ear infection, in her infant years, left her without the ability to hear, hence, she never learned to speak. She did, however, attend The Southern California Institute for the Deaf in Riverside, California where she learned sign language and lip reading. These invaluable communicative skills, out of necessity, were passed on to Debra.

Signing was something Debra doesn't ever remember not knowing. "It's second nature and comes automatically," she always explained to her childhood friends, "I've been doing it all my life." Even when speaking with someone who was not hearing impaired, she found herself signing. "Sorry," she would apologize, "force of habit."

As a child Debra had a slight speech impediment which made her the center of many cruel childhood jokes and the target for teasing by schoolyard bullies. "I'd rather be signing than speaking," she confided in her speech therapist. "The other kids always make fun of me when I speak."

By the time she was in middle school she had overcome the impediment and the teasing gradually disappeared.

At the age of twenty-six Debra was quite proficient in American Sign Language. Her knowledge, speed, and accuracy put her in high demand to serve as an interpreter for the deaf at conferences, in local church functions, and at court trials. Debra never considered her mother's condition a disability. However, she was quite aware that it was because of her mom's limitations that doors opened, giving her the opportunity to learn and use this remarkable gift to her advantage.

She often thought of the gift as *my special blessing*. "It's a *blessing* to be able to communicate for those in a world of silence. Interpreting for them makes living, in a primarily world of hearing, an easier and friendlier world," she once explained at a seminar.

"It's certainly is a pleasant brisk spring morning," she shared with her mom. "Everything is turning green and the flowers are starting to bloom. There are robins, blue jays, mockingbirds, and busy squirrels scurrying about," she described the surroundings to her mom who had, by this time, lost her eyesight due to complications from diabetes.

Debra reminisced about the day she introduced Jack to her mom. They were already engaged to get married but he insisted on asking Margaret's permission to marry Debra. *Always the proper gentlemen*, she thought.

Margaret still had her eyesight and her beautiful colorful eyes misted up as Jack nervously asked for Debra's hand in marriage. After stumbling through his request, he looked up at his future mother-in-law and blurted out, "You have the most beautiful sapphire-blue eyes."

Still blushing, Margaret laughed and replied, "You young man, are more than welcome into this family."

From that day on Jack always complimented her on her appearance. In return Margaret always responded with a smile and blushing glow.

During the weeks that ensued, Margaret and Jack developed a strong bond. Jack was the son that Margaret never had and she in turn became the mother he lost during his infant years.

"Debra, I sure hope you and Jack never go through the anguish and hurt feelings of breaking up, or even worse, go through a divorce," her mom signed. "It would break my heart if that ever happened to you two."

◘ ◘ ◘

"It seems like ages since we last had that conversation," Debra signed to her Mom.

In reality, only twelve months had passed.

Here again, at her faithful weekly visit with her mom, Debra started to show signs of nervousness and repeatedly brushed away her hair, while gently tugging on her earlobe. She spoke rapidly without really concentrating on her immediate surroundings. Between sentences she hummed a made up song, which bought her time while she gathered her thoughts.

If she had quirks left over from her childhood days, this was it. She was feeling uncomfortable and was on the verge of confessing something. Sitting on the bench, under the large elm tree, she finally blurted out and simultaneously signed, "I missed my period Mom. On my way home I'm stopping at Smith's Corner Drug Store to buy one of those pregnancy test kits. I've never used them before. I guess they're fairly accurate. Otherwise, they would've been pulled off the market by now."

There was a long pause with audible sniffles intermittently breaking the stillness of the crisp cool morning air. "That's not all," she said, her voice trembling, "Jack and I broke up. He moved out of the apartment yesterday. He's not aware that I might be pregnant. Right now, I don't want him knowing either way. If the test is positive I prefer to keep it just between you and me. I don't want him to come back just because I'm pregnant. Do you think that's dumb?"

Debra jumped up and paced a few seconds. "Raising a child without Jack shouldn't be difficult. You did great as a single mom. I only hope I can be half as good as you were." Debra glanced at her watch, "Gosh, I've got to go. I'm scheduled to interpret a case at the courthouse in an hour. Love you mom," she signed as she rushed off.

Two days later Debra returned with the results. "The test was positive. I'm pretty sure I'm having a baby." Quietly sobbing she somehow managed to express her innermost feelings, "I'm sorry you won't be able to see nor hear your grandchild. I wish you could. My appointment with the doctor is next week. She'll probably put me on a special diet, prescribe supplemental vitamins, and tell me to give up my daily glass of wine. No doubt the same advice you were given when you were carrying me."

Immediately after her doctor's appointment, she went to visit and talk with her mom. "It's official. The doctor confirmed what we already knew. You are going to be a grandmother. How do you feel about that, *Grandma?*"

Nine months later, Debra was introducing baby Eddie to his grandmother. "Mom, he has those beautiful sapphire-blue eyes and that blazing red hair, just like you."

When Eddie was one month old, Debra found herself sitting at her mom's place. Not saying nor signing a single word. She just sat there in utter silence. Unaware of her actions, she broke into the hair, earlobe, and humming routine. Her mom had learned years ago, when Debra was a toddler, that this was a prelude to some earth shattering announcement.

"There's something I've been meaning tell you," Debra, surprised herself at the loudness of her own voice, "Jack and I are back together. We've been seeing a marriage counselor. There are issues on both sides that need to be resolved. We're working on them. Anyway, we think it would be better to salvage the marriage and provide Eddie with a normal family life. I never thought I would be making decisions like these but I guess it's all part of growing up and facing life head-on."

A couple of weeks passed before Debra visited again. "Guess what? Jack got orders for overseas. He was selected to serve as the military attaché to the American Ambassador in Italy. We've been packing and processing the final documents for the trip. That's why I haven't been able to visit. It's a four year tour with a guaranteed reassignment back to a base of his choice."

Debra lingered a few minutes longer, mostly in dead silence while she cradled her sleeping Eddie. She then stood, looked around at the beautiful landscaped grounds, and let out a long slow sigh. She gently ran her free hand over the cold marble headstone and with tears in her eyes signed, "I love you Mom."

THE CRUISE

*On a cruise the co-workers sailed,
bought on-line, a bargain they nailed.
While exploring the ship at their leisure,
they met the Captain whose actions,
are exposed here, for your pleasure.*

—*R. Quero*

The Cruise

It's not unusual for co-workers to take vacations together. But what was a bit out of the norm was how this group of employees, from a New Orleans based casino, acquired the cruise. During their lunch break Audrey and Suzie jumped on the computer in pursuit of their favorite past time. Half of their salaries, if the truth be told, were spent on jewelry they purchased through ez2buy2sell.com, cheap4upeople.com, or some other online website.

"Yes, yes, yes," an excited Suzie jumped up and down elated that she had just struck gold. She had been bidding on a two-hundred dollar gold ring and after five minutes won the bid for a mere ninety dollars. While she was reveling in her victory, Audrey also won a bid for a pair of Black Hills Gold earrings. "They have just the right hint of color and I'm trying to get a necklace that matches," she announced, "and I got them for just thirteen dollars. Not bad."

They also searched jewelryforbid.com for more mind boggling deals and then decided to check out vacationsRcheap.com. A cruise aboard a newly renovated cruise liner caught their attention. The historical liner's seaworthy status was upgraded one level and was now considered one of the fastest and best equipped liners in its class. Renamed *The Norwegian Viking*, it was scheduled to make its maiden voyage, from Miami to Cozumel, on an eight days/seven nights round trip cruise.

"I can't believe this. It's only priced at $100 per person," Audrey, amazed at the unbelievable deal, kept reading out loud. "No bidding is allowed, strictly first come, first serve. This offer expires at 1 P.M."

"We only have twenty minutes to act on this deal," Suzie pointed out.

Audrey and Suzie scrambled to make phone calls to other co-workers and friends. "You don't want to pass this up,' they kept telling everyone. Within ten minutes they had a few others that agreed to sail with them.

The plan was for Audrey to put everything on her credit card and later be reimbursed. They went back on-line and were able to secure enough tickets for those that wanted to be included on this remarkably, good deal.

It was later discovered that a wealthy attorney from Florida relinquished one dozen non-transferable and non-refundable tickets. The date for his client's retrial was changed and now the case fell during the week of the scheduled cruise. The entire staff in the law firm, for whom the vacation was a gift, had to prepare and be available to represent their client in a high profile case.

Since the law firm had paid for the non-refundable cruise tickets in advance, the liner's corporate office was only charging $100 to cover the cost of paperwork associated with the cruise liner's regulations.

When Suzie received the confirmation and the boarding passes, she was pleasantly surprise to learn that each individual in the entire group would have their own private quarters. She quickly called all those that had signed up, and broke the good news, "Guess what? We're all traveling first class."

◻ ◻ ◻

Most of the group flew into Miami the night before the cruise. They all agreed to meet at Pier 34 the morning of the cruise to check-in their luggage and board as a group.

"Has any one seen Audrey or Suzie?" Tammy asked.

"They took a later flight yesterday and were diverted into Atlanta because of severe thunderstorms," Stan told his co-workers. "Suzie texted me about half an hour ago and said they were starting their descent into the Miami area."

"How about checking-in our luggage and then having breakfast at that restaurant, at the end of the pier. We still have two hours before we have to board. Maybe they'll be here by then," Lance suggested.

"Good idea," agreed Tammy, "I'm starved."

At the Dockside Café, they were seated by a window which afforded them a spectacular view of the bay and the ship that would be their home for the next eight days.

"Nice view," Linda commented, "Hope the weather clears up a little before we make sail. But just in case, I brought some motion-sickness patches for the voyage."

"Me too," everyone else confessed.

Currently, the weather was overcast with the water a bit choppy. The splash of the four foot waves against the helm of the ship created colorful rainbows as the spray from the salt water showed off its allusive color spectrum. The forecast called for borderline inclement weather the first night at sea with the remainder of the week slated as clear sailing. "These four-footers are nothing compared to what we'll be sailing through, even in calm seas," Lance warned the group.

They waited as long as they could before boarding the ship. "I feel bad boarding without Audrey and Suzie," Tammy said, "It's as if we're abandoning them. After all, they're the ones that made the trip possible."

"Don't worry about those two," Robert assured her, "Knowing them as long as I have, I'm sure they'll find a way to make it on time. Come on let's go. The last call to board has already been announced over the PA system."

"Let's make our way to one of the decks where the festivities are being held and we can watch as the ship is towed to open waters," recommended Linda.

Making their way through the crowd of vacationers, they were showered with confetti and streamers. On every level of the ship live *mariachi* or *calypso* music filled the air, giving them a small taste of a fun filled week they would enjoy during the upcoming week. All the passengers were at the railings waving and shouting their goodbyes to those on shore. The small group of casino employees were also waving and yelling, not at friends or loved ones who had come to bid them *bon voyage*, but to Audrey and Suzie who were running down the pier trying to board the ship preparing to make sail.

"HURRY, HURRY," they yelled, with the loud noise produced by the reveling passengers drowning out their voices.

To Audrey and Suzie's good fortune, the filming of VIPs boarding the liner delayed the hoisting of the gangplank. The two, late passengers, were able to scurry on board in the nick of time. In their haste they left their luggage at the terminal and rushed past security and the VIPs.

They were immediately apprehended and taken aside for questioning. After confirmation that they were not stowaways or terrorists, they were given a lengthy reprimand and an in-depth lecture on safety and security.

"Does everyone get this sort of treatment and lecturing," they inquired of the security officers.

"No, but it isn't everyday people storm pass security and rudely shove their way pass the governor and his family. We're actually letting you off lightly."

The embarrassed and apologetic duo was finally released and able to join their friends. Arrangements were made to have their luggage put on a helicopter, scheduled to make a routine flight later that evening.

◘ ◘ ◘

The first planned activity was a getting-to-know-you party that evening. It was a "come as you are" gathering and was the only time that alcoholic beverages would be provided "free of charge". "Call it what you like, but I call it an ice-breaker with free drinks," said Lance, grinning as he took the small paper umbrella out of his Mai Tai and stuck it in his thick wavy red hair. "This Long Island Iced Tea is delicious and need I add, quite potent," Robert let it be known. "Yeah, and the food isn't all that bad either," Suzie added.

The evening's event went far into the wee hours. There were people from every walk of life and every conceivable profession. The night was spent nibbling on a vast array of food served at the buffet tables, mingling with the rest of the vacationers, and line dancing to Latin, country, and the golden oldies.

It was a pleasantly cool and breezy night. The liner's course skirted the edge of the weather front, keeping it on the fair side. Half of the party goers moseyed out on the deck enjoying the refreshing salt air.

Tammy, who was trying to keep up with Suzie's dancing asked, "Where in the world do you get all that energy?"

"The secret is to dance five songs and then take a breather for two or three songs," replied Suzie. "That way you can make it through the night without pooping out."

"Goodness," commented Audrey, "I didn't know you were such a good dancer."

"I can hold my own . . . most of the time," Suzie replied, "But I have to admit, I could only go three songs against the cloggers from Ireland. All that hard stomping made my feet feel like they were beaten with a meat tenderizer. I think, maybe, that another martini might help kill the pain."

Working her way through the crowd on the promenade deck Linda was bumped by a couple that was dancing and caused her to spill red wine on her silk blouse. "Just splash some club soda on it and let it soak," the barmaid kindly advised.

"Linda, that actually works. The soda will neutralize the wine stain," a male voice pitched in. Linda spun around to see who else was dispensing laundry tips at her. It was Stan, who just happened to be working his way back to his room. Lance and Robert were right behind him. They too were calling it quits.

Lance, who obviously had thoroughly enjoyed the night was now sporting a dozen umbrellas and was working on his thirteenth. "Puth thum shoda on yur blouth," he slurred, as Robert helped him steady his walk.

The majority of the partiers were also calling it a night. It seemed that the long day and first long night, not to mention the flow of free booze, had everyone exhausted and, some literally, wiped out.

The first full day at sea promised to be full of activities with breakfast being offered from 6:30 A.M. thru 10:00 A.M. But at this very moment, the only thing on everyone's minds was some long overdue shut eye.

Although several activities were made available, most of the passengers took time after breakfast to explore the various levels of the ship. The upper deck housed the cabanas and the swimming pool. This is where Lance and Suzie decided to recover from their splitting hangovers while showing off their new thongs. Located at the other end of the top deck was the driving range and shuffle board area.

Later that evening, while enjoying a beverage at 'The Deck Bar', Stan boasted, "I hit a record 300 golf balls into the Gulf of Mexico. You should've seen the dolphins chasing after the balls as they splashed into the wake created by the ship. They were swallowing the balls as fast as I could hit them."

Audrey, a staunch environmentalist and proponent for protection against cruelty to animals, sat up in her seat and started wagging her finger at him. "You should know better than that, Stan. You and those other golfers should not have been hitting those balls into the water. Marine life has enough problems surviving without humans adding garbage, trash, and manufactured golf balls to their diets."

"The golf balls are made of a special compound derived strictly from fish byproducts and considered a good source of supplemental nourishment for the dolphins," Stan informed her.

Having to swallow her pride, Audrey apologized, "Sorry for jumping to conclusions. You know how strongly I feel about animal rights. Next time I might even join you and hit a few treats to those playful sea mammals."

"Then I guess we have a date at sea. We'll have a ball," punned Stan.

The next day Linda called Tammy, Suzie, and Audrey. "How about we do some more exploring of the ship without the guys?"

"Not me," Audrey told her. "Stan and I have reservations at the driving range."

After forty-five minutes of walking up and down stairs and roaming through long narrow passageways Linda, Tammy, and Suzie heard piano music softly flowing through the corridors of the deck on which they were snooping.

"It's coming from over there," Linda said, pointing to an open door at the end of the long hallway. "Let's see if they'll allow us to sit and listen," she suggested.

They followed the melodic sounds to what appeared to be a small recreation room. A stately looking gentleman, in a crisp white uniform, was sitting with his back to the entrance playing a baby grand.

"Excuse us. May we sit and listen to you play?" they asked.

Startled, he spun around and blushed with embarrassment. "I didn't know anyone else was down here. I was just tinkering on the keyboard. It's one of my favorite past times."

He apologized for his mediocre talent and introduced himself as the ship's captain. "I am Captain Jorgensen and I must confess that I periodically sneak away from my duties to practice my music."

They introduced themselves and explained that they were just checking out the ship.

"I'm surprised that you even found this small game room, since it's tucked away in an obscure corner of the ship."

The Captain gave them a quick rundown on the history of the baby grand and the harpsichord in the room. "This harpsichord," he shared as he sat to play it, "was given by a distant cousin of Amadeus Mozart. He too was a musician but at the time lacked the funds to travel abroad. In return for passage fare and extra spending money, Mozart's relative traded this beautiful work of art. The plans are to donate these instruments to the Museum of Music, in Austria."

Switching from one instrument to the other he indulged them on requests for a small taste of classical masterpieces.

All three ladies were immediately spell bound by his deep baritone accent and his striking good looks. They later agreed that his music was also captivating.

The Captain turned out to be quite an accomplished pianist with an intriguing background. "I was born in Oslo and graduated from a very elite music conservatory in Europe. After six years of touring, as a concert pianist, I was offered a position as a member of the Royal Symphonic Orchestra of Norway."

As he played the piano he told them, "In order to fulfill my obligations to my country, I joined the Norwegian Royal Navy as a commissioned officer. It was then that I fell in love with the sea and the vessels that sail the waters of the globe."

"Upon completion of my military service," he continued, "I put my training and experience to good use, by seeking employment with the shipping industry. Working my way through the ranks, I was eventually promoted to Captain, and assigned to this vessel."

Captain Jorgensen then took the time to show them an old, but mint condition, phonograph. "This phonograph is the original record player that was in the officer's mess in the 1930's". "It still plays quite well," he said, "I especially like the nostalgic look and the rich resonant sound it produces."

"Let me show you the rest of this deck," the Captain offered. "This level is what we call the 'boat deck'. The deck below is the Promenade, which is made up of first class state rooms, a first class lounge, and a small library. The boat deck consists, primarily, of the radio room, a small recreation room, a gymnasium, the officers' quarters and a small officers' dining room, which we call the *mess*."

As they stepped back into the recreation room he pointed at a closed door at the far end of the corridor, "Through that door is the *bridge*," he informed them.

"I'd like to play you a piece I've thought up. I'll name it *A Piece for Three Lovely Ladies*," he told them as he sat at the piano. In the short time they were together, Captain Jorgensen had composed a short melody in their honor. Mesmerizing them with his seductive presentation, his long fingers gracefully stroked the ivory keys. The young ladies, figuratively speaking, melted in their seats.

Suzie, Linda, and Tammy didn't realize he had already finished playing, when he asked them, "Did you ladies enjoy the impromptu piece?"

The trio was speechless and embarrassed to have been caught up into such a state of passion. They found themselves stammering before Linda spoke up for the three of them. "Captain Jorgensen, we're having a great time, but we have selfishly used up so much of your busy day. You're a wonderful host and an extremely talented pianist. We'll remember this as the most favorite part of this cruise."

"Believe me, I've enjoyed every minute. And please don't feel like you wasted my time. It's all been good therapy for me. I consider my playing as a mechanism which helps release stress brought on by my duties as Captain. I should be the one thanking you all for being part of my therapy. It gave me a chance to brush off the old cobwebs, and to share a tune or two with you beautiful ladies. I'm sure that you'll encounter many more memorable moments on this ship. Please have a great time and enjoy the rest of the cruise," he bowed slightly as he politely dismissed himself.

Returning back to their state rooms to freshen up, they couldn't stop talking about the time and attention devoted to them by "their" Captain. It was obvious that Captain Jorgensen's tall and muscular stature, his deep blue eyes, and charismatic personality had swept all three off their feet.

They couldn't wait to share their afternoon with the rest of the group. There was no way that anyone of their friends could have had a better afternoon then the one they had just experienced.

▫ ▫ ▫

The next day at noon, the random selection of ten guests were picked to dine at The Captain's Table the following evening. It was the cruise's formal dinner function that everyone was looking forward to and were all hyped up about.

By pure coincidence, the three ladies' names were drawn. "What luck! Can you believe it? We're sitting at The Captain's Table," they screamed with enthusiasm.

"I wonder if Captain Jorgensen had any bearing or input on us being selected? After all he did say we would encounter more memorable moments," Suzie wondered out loud.

"Maybe he somehow finagled it so that we were picked as guests of honor at his table," Linda said.

"I don't care how it came about. I'm just glad we were picked. But if any of the passengers get wind of it, they might be upset that he was exercising preference. We better not mention the personal time Captain Jorgensen spent with us," Tammy advised her friends.

The girls spent the next afternoon at the beauty parlor getting their hair, nails, and facials done. Everyone had brought evening wear for the, well publicized, formal affair; but not one of them had anticipated sitting at The Captain's Table. What an honor it was. No one was more nervous, yet more tickled pink, than this excited threesome.

The evening started with a small combo playing light jazz during the cocktail hour with a pay-as-you go bar. The vacationers mingled enjoying the music, drinks, and hors d'oeuvres.

The Cruise Director took the podium to make an announcement.

"Ladies and gentlemen may I have your attention! First, I want to thank you all for coming to the Captain's Formal Dinner Party. I trust you are enjoying the wonderful beverages and delectable hors d'oeuvres. Unfortunately, the Captain is detained with his duties, so will not be able to attend the cocktail hour. But he wants to extend his welcome to all of you and says he will see you at the dinner hour. Thank you!"

When the dinner bell rang at 6:00 P.M. the guests were all ushered into the banquet room. It was open seating for everyone except those seated at the Captain's Table. The ten lucky people were assigned their seats. Conveniently, as the young ladies deduced, they had the seats closest to Captain Jorgensen. "Not a word, girls," Tammy whispered under her breath, making eye contact with Suzie and Linda.

After all the dinner guests had been seated and before the first course of the meal was served the Maître d' announced "Ladies and gentleman . . . Captain Lloyd Zachary." Everyone stood and applauded his entrance. The trio was stunned. *Could their Captain Jorgensen be ill or too busy to attend the night's events?* They mulled over several reasons in their minds, as the gears in their heads went into overtime, working to solve the mystery.

"Thank you, please be seated." Zachary instructed the dinner guests, with a heavy unrecognizable accent. "First of all let me apologize for not being able to attend the cocktail hour. Some unforeseen business required my attention. I hope you enjoyed yourselves and find the remainder of the evening just as pleasant."

Before taking his seat, he commenced getting acquainted with the guests of honor at his table by going to each guest and briefly getting to know them. He started with the guests at the far end of the table and worked his way to those nearest him. Captain Zachary came across just as charming and as polite as Captain Jorgensen.

The noise level in the banquet room gradually diminished from a low roar to a soft buzz as the dinner guests indulged in mouth-watering crab bisque, succulent lobster, rack of lamb, steamed vegetables, and an assortment of rich decadent desserts.

Meanwhile, the suspicious and inquisitive trio had a chance to converse. "I know he seems like a kind person," Linda pointed out, "but I smell foul play."

"Captain Jorgensen is being held hostage or maybe even removed from the ship," Tammy shared her theory with her cohorts, adding fuel to their unfolding mystery plot.

""Yeah," Suzie filled them in, "I heard some unscheduled arrivals and departures of helicopters and large motor boats."

"And don't forget all those gunshots?" Linda reminded them.

"It seems to me like it might be an act of clandestine piracy involving this cruise liner," Tammy concluded.

"Shh! He's looking in our direction," Suzie alerted them.

"Ladies," the Captain addressed them as they tried to look calm. "I haven't had the honor of meeting you. My table roster has you listed as Tammy and you as Suzie. That means that you must be Linda," he said, as he politely made eye contact with each one and slightly nodded his head in recognition.

Tammy kept making faces at Linda, the self-proclaimed ring leader, giving her a queue to raise the issue at hand. Unable to contain her curiosity any longer and trying hard to act nonchalant, Linda inquired,

"Sir, will Captain Jorgensen be joining us for dinner or is he indisposed for the night?"

"I'm afraid I don't follow you," Zachary answered back, with an apparent waver in his voice.

The girls also detected a light nervous twitch over his right eye, as he nervously stroked his neatly trimmed Van Dyke. At this point, their suspicions were confirmed. Hoping not to alarm the rest of the cruisers, thus averting chaos, they quietly asked to speak with him in private. Acting annoyed, yet diplomatic, he politely accepted their unusual request. "Let's step out into the grand foyer," he suggested.

Trailing the Captain, Suzie whispered to her comrades," Be careful he might try to have us abducted."

"Now what is this all about?" he requested to know.

They explained to Zachary, "While exploring the ship, we met the 'real' Captain. He unselfishly spent time playing the harpsichord and piano for us. Captain Jorgensen gave us a personal tour of the ship's boat deck and arranged for us to be seated at the Captain's Table."

"We also heard all the activity with the helicopter and boats coming and going. We know there's something fishy going on. And we want to know what you've done with Captain Jorgensen and his officers."

Captain Zachary appeared slightly uneasy as he chuckled and grinned. "Ladies I appreciate your sense of humor. But when this ship was renovated, the part of the deck in question was turned into a storage area. You would have to know the combination to the double doors to access that area. As for the allegations pertaining to 'piracy on the high seas', as you perceive it," he said with a smirk on his face, "You probably heard the helicopter that transported the Governor and his family, due to personal matters, back to the state capital."

"What about the gun fire? What was all that about? Linda further drilled him.

"We routinely fire shots prior to the helicopters landing or departing the helo pad. The noise scares off the sea gulls. Birds and aircrafts don't make a good combination. If they get sucked in through the intake manifold it could cause the engines to stall." Now, is this the extent of this *shenanigan* of yours or do you have other pressing issues that require my immediate attention?"

Noticing the blank expressions on their faces, Captain Zachary told the three women, "Ladies, I didn't mean to sound rude or disrespectful, but you must realize how insane this notion of yours sounds."

After a few seconds of awkward silence, Captain Zachary smartly snapped his heels and bowed to them. "Please excuse me, but I have a dining room full of guests I have neglected all night."

Obviously irritated, yet partially amused, he left them standing in the grand and majestic foyer. He walked a few steps, stopped and looked back over his shoulder, "You ladies didn't really hear Jorgensen play the piano. I suspect that the three of you visited the ship's museum and read that in 1932 Captain Jorgensen, an accomplished musician and womanizer, died at sea after a bout with malaria. "Good evening ladies."

Speechless, dumbfounded, and terribly shaken, the trio spent the rest of the night at the piano bar.

THE LIFE OF
LU WANG

***A** man on a boat from Shanghai,*
befriended a short but nice guy.
They opened a restaurant, sit-in or take out,
and deliveries, with rice piled high.

—*R. Quero*

The Life of Lu Wang

Dexter Quinn had mixed emotions about his last meeting with Lu Wang. This was the thirtieth, and last, face-to-face interview with Mr. Wang. The meetings were for one hour, every Sunday morning, for thirty weeks. During the past twenty-nine hours he had asked more questions and learned more about this one man's life than any other person he had ever met. He had developed a close and special bond with Lu, as Mr. Wang preferred to be called. The bond, more than likely, stemmed from the fact that Lu had literally opened his heart and shared his entire life with Dexter. The good, the bad, and the ugly . . . it was, as Dexter trusted, the whole truth of this remarkable old man's life.

"Mr. Wang," Dexter explained his intentions, "The premise for the interviews is to gather firsthand information, to be used in a series of biographical documentaries featuring a myriad of cultures that are interwoven into the culture of the America as we know it today. These particular strings of documentaries will focus on Chinese immigrants who settled in the coastal regions of Southern California in the mid 1940's and went on to become influential pillars in their communities. Would you mind being part of this documentary?"

Mr. Wang humbly agreed, "As long as a portion of the profits from these hour long interviews are donated for the refurbishment of the Asian Cultural Arts Center (ACAC), then I will grant you the interviews."

The center was a model project that many cities emulated and one that, from its conception through its present day existence, was spearheaded by Lu Wang himself. The entire operation of the ACAC was strictly funded by private donations, revenue from functions, exhibitions, and lease of space in this state-of-the-art facility.

At times Dexter felt uncomfortable asking personal and often invasive questions. Although Mr. Wang was heavily involved and highly respected in the community, he was also a very private person. But to get to the core of what this man was made of and how he helped shape the local community, Dexter had to pry into the personal life and dig into the deepest areas of this man's soul.

Mr. Wang, on the other hand, felt perfectly at ease. It was, in essence, an oral autobiography, that he was sharing with Dexter and who else would be able to do it better, than Lu himself?

Dexter's brain was bombarded with questions. *What made Lu Wang the person he was? What things in the course of his life influenced him? Who did he consider the mentors in his life? How did he pick which projects or goals to pursue and support? And probably the most important questions were: If given the opportunity, what would you change about your life?"* and *"Are there any regrets?"*

"If I pose the questions just right and if the answers are pertinent and informative, then I am convinced that I will be able to do justice to the documentary, to the viewing public, and to Mr. Wang," Dexter informed his producers.

To every interview, Mr. Wang wore the traditional Chinese mandarin collared shirt with the knot buttons and a pair of baggy cotton pants. Today, for the last interview and to honor Dexter Quinn, Lu Wang chose to wear a colorful, formal Chinese outfit made of silk with a hand embroidered pattern. At seventy-five years of age he carried himself with dignity, with his head held high, and with a posture straight and erect. His very being and appearance radiated pride in his oriental heritage. He was about five foot, eight inches in height and weighed, roughly about one hundred and seventy pounds. Even in the loose Chinese attire, one could see that for a man his age, he was in good physical condition.

His legendary past as a *Kung Fu* master coupled with his highly revered status in the community was intimidating and, at first, was met with slight trepidation on Dexter's part. He spoke perfect English, albeit he still carried a slight touch of his Chinese accent. Dexter had only spoken with Mr. Wang twice on the phone, at which time they both came to a mutual agreement (with the approval of legal authorities) on the setting, format, and time restraints regarding the interviews.

"In person, Mr. Wang turned out to be an extremely polite and very cordial individual. Quite the opposite of what I envisioned him being," Dexter shared with his colleagues.

The interviews themselves turned out to be a lot easier than what Dexter had expected. Arriving with a notebook full of questions, Dexter at first thought it would be like pulling teeth. Because of the current circumstances and the newsworthy events unfolding in Lu Wang's life, he was under the impression that Mr. Wang would only be giving single word responses or at the very most, short sentence replies to the questions asked. Contrary to Dexter's preconceived notions Lu Wang took one or two questions and literally ran with them; explaining everything in detail, describing every person in the unfolding sagas, and reliving the incredible journey his life had taken.

Dexter remembered trying to relax in the stiff chair with the hard-padded seat during the first interview. He looked at Lu Wang straight in the eyes and blurted out, "Tell me Mr. Wang, who you are, where you came from and about your early life as a boy."

"Please call me Lu", the old Asian requested as he sat back, thought for a moment and in a somber voice set the scene for the beginning of his life's story.

"It's been so many years, so much has happened. Yet it seems like just yesterday." This was Lu Wang's introduction into the fascinating and unique life that spanned nearly eight decades.

"Throughout the entire thirty interviews, Lu kept me mesmerized with explicit details, colorful anecdotes, and a roller coaster ride of interesting, personal and, at times, emotional experiences," Dexter later wrote.

▫ ▫ ▫

"I never knew who my parents were. The monks at the *Tao* Temple told me that I was left at the main entrance to the temple on a cold wintery night. When the tall twenty foot gates to the main entrance were closed the night prior, the streets were abandoned. Surely, no one was fool enough to be out on that cold, snowy night. But at the crack of dawn, when the gates were opened to allow early worshippers access to the temple, a baby was found outside the gates. The newborn swaddled in strips of dirty, stained cotton cloths was left in a basket covered with a large piece of *yak* wool to protect it from the frigid winter temperatures. That baby was me. The basket I was in was placed with other baskets containing vegetables and fish donated by the local farmers to help feed the monks and as offerings to the deities."

The monks later told me, "A note, which was hastily scribbled in Chinese characters, simply read, 'Take care of baby'. A set of small footprints, almost completely covered by the windswept snow, led up to the temple gates and retreated in the same direction from whence they came."

The two monks, responsible for opening the gates, immediately took me inside. After rescuing me from the inclement weather they, along with their fellow brethren, made sure that my immediate needs were properly addressed. From the condition of the umbilical cord, it was estimated that their abandoned baby was probably no older than a week and for obvious reasons and to the monks' relief, it was noted that I was a boy."

After several days of inquiring and searching for the baby's parents or relatives the monks came to the conclusion that either no one knew who the baby belonged to or no one was willing to readily give out the information. Perhaps the baby was originally from another province and was simply abandoned by passing sojourners.

The baby left in the street was found by *Lu* and *Wang*. Destiny played a role in these monks being assigned to open the temple gates that wintery morning. It was meant to happen as it did and the monks of the *Tao* Temple were not in the position to go against the course that divine forces had put into motion.

"The eldest monk's name was *Wang* and was bestowed the honors of giving his surname to the baby. The name *Wang* derives from an area from which some ancient Chinese dynasties originated. It literally means 'prince'," Lu Wang told the interviewer.

"The younger monk's surname was *Lu*. *Lu* was the name of a an area in China that is currently known as *Shandong* Province. Through interpretation and rewriting of the Chinese character representing the word *lu*, it has come to be translated as one of several words for "street". All the monks of the *Tao* Temple believed that the sequence of events, leading up to that point, dictated that the baby, from that day forth, be known as . . . *Lu Wang*," the former monk gave Dexter a few seconds to write notes on the origin of his name.

"Prince of the street, can you believe that?" He laughed as he recalled the story. "Or is it Street Prince? Who knows?" he said revealing the lighter side of his character. Nevertheless, that's how the monks told me I got my name," Lu laughed, as he leaned back, giving himself a chance to catch his thoughts before continuing with his life's story.

"I suppose I should be grateful that I was a male baby and not a female. Otherwise the monks might have handed me over to the orphanage run by the British missionaries," Wang quipped.

"My childhood was unique, to say the least. I was raised by sixty monks. I was, for all practical purposes, brought up by sixty dads. I was forever being disciplined and corrected on the spot. It seemed that every move I made, every corner I turned, and every breath I took was seen or heard by one of the monks. They were my parents, my playmates, my educators, and my disciplinarians. They were a major part of my life as much as I was of theirs," the old man smiled as he reminisced and silently savored those childhood days, so long ago.

Lu Wang was raised in the strict ways of the *Taoist* monks. When old enough to understand and to put into practice the various concepts of their philosophy, he was then appropriately instructed. As a young lad he spent countless hours with individual monks, learning from them and practicing their Asian rituals. He was taught the basics of life: Cleanliness, respect for all mankind, and to acknowledge and protect all forms of life. He was also taught to be self-sufficient by learning gardening, cooking, and tailoring. He was brought up believing that human beings should live in harmony with nature and that a prolonged and honorable life should be sought after.

"The monks told me that before I could even stand up and walk, I was seen trying to mimic the movements as they practiced *San Soo Kung Fu*, an ancient form of the martial arts. By the age of six I was working out with them the entire two hours four times a week. I was limber, agile, and lightning fast. The challenges *Kung Fu* offered were more than welcomed. When my daily regimen of duties permitted, I would practice several hours on my own. In time I mastered the use of the martial arts primitive, yet effective, weapons."

"*Kung Fu* increased my confidence, improved my balance, and sharpened my senses. I could hear, see, and sense my opponent's presence and learned to accurately anticipate their every move. I learned to use and control my strength, and like a tiger, was able to leap heights, unlike my dads' capabilities. The speed that my arms and legs rendered was remarkable. My movements were powerful, yet executed with the gracefulness of a floating butterfly. Of course now, Dexter, I am not quite as fast and agile as when I was a young lad."

As Dexter found out, another art that Lu Wang was taught was *Shan shui*. "*Shan shui* is an art form in which a brush and ink is used instead of the more conventional paints. This form of art showed it's prominence in Chinese history during the 5th century," Lu explained.

"I thoroughly enjoyed the inner peace that I felt when I spent time inking scenes of natural landscapes. The mountains, rivers, and waterfalls are part of nature that I was taught to respect. I was honored to be able to depict their existence through brush and ink. I spent so much time using my brush and ink set that for years my fingers were dyed grayish black," shared Lu Wang, with a chuckle.

"Of all the things that those sixty dads passed on to me the art of *Kung Fu* and the art of *Shan shui* were the two that I cherished the most." Lu's eyes twinkled when he shared with Dexter his formative years and the roles these two ancient and graceful art forms contributed to the development of his own character.

"When I turned eight years of age, I was enrolled in a school run by the same British organization that ran the orphanage. The monks felt that I should learn English and believed that exposure to a foreign culture would be beneficial for a well-rounded education."

Through the eyes and books, of these missionaries, the young Chinese lad learned of cultures unlike the only one he had ever known. He learned of various social and political structures; of flavorful and exotic cuisines; and of the different religions practiced across this globe.

Mr. Wang told Dexter that he was highly intrigued with the foreign languages. "I quickly picked up English, German, and Spanish. As I grew into my teenage years, I was expected to pull my share of night guard on the temple grounds and would often be heard patrolling the grounds, talking to myself in one language and responding in a different one."

Ten Twists

▫ ▫ ▫

Shortly after his eighteenth birthday Lu Wang approached his dads about traveling abroad. "I have been completely fascinated with the stories of western cultures taught to me by the missionaries and I have made up my mind. Even as a child I knew that one day I would travel to distant lands. I think," I told my adopted family, expressing my desires, "America would be an excellent country to visit." Although his dads were not keen on the idea of Lu Wang leaving, they also were aware that he was a young man and could not be held against his will. Lu Wang was at the age of choosing, on his own, whether he wished to remain and live as part of the temple family, live outside the walls of the temple, or possibly even travel beyond the territories of China. Lu Wang chose the latter.

The monks made arrangements for Lu Wang to sail on a freight liner. They paid an initial fee and it was agreed that Lu Wang would work as a cabin boy, for the officers on the ship, in exchange for room and board. His dads supplied Lu Wang with extra traveling clothes, some food, and some money to help him get settled in America.

It was an emotional farewell. All the monks, the missionaries, the students, and the majority of the villagers were on hand when Lu Wang set off on his journey. He travelled five days, on foot, before he reached the coastal town of *Shanghai* where he was to set sail.

Upon arrival to the Port of *Shanghai* he found out that a slot did not exist for an extra cabin boy nor was there space for additional passengers. No one in the position of authority was aware of, nor did anyone have a record of any pre-arranged travel agreements. "Welcome to *Shanghai*. We're sorry but you have been swindled," was the best the ship's company could come up with.

After hearing his story, some Chinese dock workers helped sneak him onto the ship in an empty pickle barrel. Once on board he would be on his own to prevent being detected and caught. "Stowaways," he was warned, "are severely punished by the officials and incarcerated under extremely harsh conditions."

"My first two nights were uneventful. I hid in the cargo area where barrels and crates of food were stored. I managed to move in and out of my hiding place during the night without detection. The ship was only out at sea for two days when I started to feel the symptoms of motion sickness. Fortunately, I was able to fight off the sensation by sitting perfectly still and concentrating on adapting to the ship's motion at sea. My training in *Kung Fu* helped him overcome and take control of my equilibrium, making the trip bearable."

On the third night, when he was hurrying to get back into his cramped and lackluster travel accommodations, he was spotted by one of the ship's supply stewards. They both froze and stared at each other.

The steward recognized the stowaway as of Chinese origin and addressed him in his language, "Don't be afraid. I won't hurt you. Who are you and what are you doing here?" the steward drilled the stowaway.

"Please help me. Don't turn me in. I am Lu Wang and am only trying to get to America," Lu Wang pleaded. He explained that he had been scammed and how the dock workers had helped him sneak on board.

The steward promised Lu Wang that he would not turn him in. He shared that he too, a couple of years earlier, was a stowaway on a ship to America. "My name is Relo Marana. I have been working on this ship for one year. Don't worry, I will help you."

Lu Wang kept staring at the steward. "I've never seen a little black man before," he was embarrassed to admit. "Where do you come from? How do you know my language?"

"I am from the Philippine Islands and come from a small tribe called Negritos. We are of small stature and of dark skin. I have worked with many people from your country and learned your language."

Relo was about four foot ten and was nineteen years old, one year older than Lu Wang. He had a very dark mahogany complexion, kinky yellowish brown hair, and a lean muscular body. His arms seemed to be proportionately longer for his height than that of a man of average size. A friendship developed between the two Asians. They soon discovered that both spoke English and were able to communicate in two languages. Throughout the voyage Relo would, at least once a day, sneak a hot meal to his new friend. "Lu Wang," Relo would constantly remind him, "you must stay well hidden down here in the bowels of the ship, so that you will not get caught. Just keep low behind the cargo so that you are not detected when the ship guards make their rounds. You'll hear them coming. They always bang their nightsticks on the crates to scare the rats."

When the ship arrived in San Pedro, California Relo made sure that Lu Wang was well hidden in an empty container that was taken on shore to be restocked with provisions for the return trip.

Having previously acquired a work visa, Relo decided not to make sail on the return voyage. Instead the two young men chose to seek employment in the "land of opportunity."

"We immediately found jobs working as stoop laborers tending the fields and harvesting the abundant California crops," Lu Wang recalled. "We worked the fields about three months averaging ten hour days, six days a week. I was surprised we even lasted that long. We thought long and hard of starting a business. We considered a laundry business, a grocery store, a shoe repair shop, and even a saloon. We didn't have any idea of how to start a business. We just knew that working as field hands was not part of our future plans."

"One day I shared my meager lunch with a couple of workers. They couldn't stop commenting and bragging to other workers how delicious and flavorful it was."

"That's it," Relo practically yelled, jabbing me with his elbow. "We can open an eatery. You know how to cook. Back at your Temple you cooked for up to sixty people."

"Dexter, we spent one week searching for a building and found one in a community known as Rivertown. It was perfect. The majority of the population was Asian and they were in dire need of a place that served oriental food."

"So with the money I had left and with the money Relo had saved from his wages as a steward, we were able to lease the bottom floor of the small two story building that once functioned as a neighborhood grocery store. The second floor was occupied by a tailor who lived and worked out of his leased space," Lu Wang shared during one of the interviews.

"We decided to convert the place into a hot meal outlet. The first floor had one cold water faucet in the front of the store and one in the back room that was once the storage area. An outlet for natural gas was also located in the storage area. Electricity was already installed. Both the front and back of the store had four light sockets hanging from six foot electric cords. These provided sufficient lighting for both areas. An in-house toilet was non-existent. All tenants, of the buildings on that same block, shared a row of five outhouses located in the alleyway. Running the length of the block, the alley divided the block in half with the backside of the buildings facing the alley. All the blocks, in this small community of immigrants, were laid out in the same manner," recalled the old man from China.

The front of the store was converted into a sit-in eatery. The place was plain but functional. The back half of the storage area was their living space. A sheet draped over a wire separated the living area from the storage and cooking section. Their kitchen consisted of four gas burners and two small sinks. One sink was used as their personal wash basin. The second sink, located next to the stoves, served to wash the cooking and eating utensils and to prep the food.

"We acquired used china and eating utensils from a restaurant that had folded and bought four Chinese cooking pans; two large and two medium size woks. We also purchased a dozen tables with chairs."

During the noon hour they delivered hot meals to the field laborers. Lu Wang, with his experience cooking for sixty family members, did the cooking. Their eatery only served Chinese food.

"The business was a joint effort," Lu Wang made sure Relo received due credit, "I shopped at the farmers market, at five in the morning every day Monday through Saturday. Relo prepped the food, and I cooked. We both delivered the food to the fields and orchards. The majority of our clientele consisted of Chinese, Japanese, and Filipino migrant workers. The meals always consisted of steamed rice and a broth type soup. On even numbered days lo mein with meat and vegetables was served, while on odd numbered days, a fish dish was cooked and served. At dinner time the eatery had a menu, scribbled on chalkboard that offered a variety of Chinese dishes. At night I prepped and cooked, and Relo waited on the customers and washed the dishes. After a few months, business was doing well enough to hire a waitress. The lady we hired was named Tomasa."

During an informal interview for the waitress position, Tomasa told them, "My mother was *mestiza,* that mean me mix of Mexican and Filipino. My father he Chinese. I speak three languages and English too. Good English," she emphasized her abilities, trying to impress the proprietors. "My husband is disabled construction worker. Me and him only live two blocks away. I have no family, so me can work extra, any time you need. Me hard worker. You see." Tomasa continued to tell them, in her stilted way of speaking English, "I work as waitress b'fore. I have experience. Know how to keep books. Do numbers."

"Yes we need someone to do our bookkeeping," Relo said. "I think we might be able to utilize your services."

"She's perfect for the job," Lu Wang happily agreed.

"When the customers, who were mostly young male immigrants, got too rowdy or had too much to drink, Tomasa would keep them in line. She was no easy push over. After their first confrontation with this strong willed, bull-headed woman, the unsuspecting customer would immediately back off. In due time, they all learned to respect and admire her tenacity. All bets on the table were for the waitress, when a newcomer tried to pull one over on her. Tomasa always came out ahead," Mr. Wang recalled, with a slight smile.

"Everyone eventually came to regard her as an older sister. She listened when they needed a lending ear and gave sound advice when they needed it. She would do anything for them and they in turn would've probably given their lives for her," he told Dexter.

Tomasa encouraged Lu Wang and Relo to go to night school and learn about America so they could become U.S. citizens. She helped many immigrants, get their citizenship papers, including Lu Wang and Relo. "USA-good country. Become citizen," she would encourage everyone. "Study booklet and do paperwork for U.S. citizenship. America good country."

"She was a good teacher. On Sundays, Relo and I allowed her to use the restaurant as a classroom to help the local immigrants prepare for their naturalization exams. She didn't charge anything. That's how strongly she felt about United States Citizenship."

"Her job at the eatery entailed waiting on the customers, making sure all take-out meals were correct, and that the noon lunches were properly packed," Dexter was told. "Several laborers, due to diet restrictions or religious beliefs, ordered special meals. I honored such requests and Tomasa made sure that all special orders were correctly labeled with the customers' names."

With Tomasa on board, Relo was free to concentrate primarily on helping prep the food. Relo and Lu Wang, however, still shared delivering the lunches during the noon hour. Xavier, Tomasa's husband, also helped deliver food, wash dishes, and keep a clean establishment.

"Once Tomasa started keeping the books, we begin seeing an increase in our profits. All the profits made by the food service went back into the business or into our individual savings. Relo and I eventually purchased the building. We made the upstairs our living quarters and the back of the restaurant was enlarged into a proper kitchen with adequate storage space. In time, hot water heaters were installed upstairs and in the restaurant.

Indoor toilet facilities were finally added and the outhouses became a thing of the past," the proud restaurateur told his interviewer.

Up to this point the place was known by all the locals as the Chinese Eatery. It had no sign out front because the place was well known. The operating license only had the address and under "Name of Business", was hand written "Chinese eatery."

The proprietors of the eating establishment were contacted by the officials from city hall and were told that for legal purposes a name for the restaurant had to be on file. After several days of trying to come up with a name, Relo finally said, "Let's just name it Lu Wang's Restaurant. People come from all over to eat the food you cook. It's Lu Wang's cooking they come for, so it should be called 'Lu Wang's Restaurant'.

"What a wonderful gesture," Lu told Dexter at the end of the hour long interview, "my friend honored me by naming our restaurant Lu Wang's."

◻ ◻ ◻

The first ten years of the restaurant's existence saw an incredible growth in business and lured patrons from far and near. When people were in the vicinity for business, or pleasure, it was Lu Wang's they made it a point to visit.

Tomasa's savvy for making business connections had Lu Wang's Restaurant delivering to two smaller restaurants located in nearby counties. They were American restaurants but every Tuesday would alternate Chinese chop suey or sweet and sour pork prepared by Lu Wang's Restaurant. The food was transported in stainless steel containers. Tomasa made sure that the proper amount ordered was sent to the right restaurants and that an extra container of steamed rice for each restaurant made it on to the delivery truck.

"Why do we always give so much rice?" Relo asked.

"Me take care of special customers," Tomasa told Relo and Lu Wang, "It called goodwill and it help pay mortgage on restaurant. Ain't that right?" she asked Xavier, as if looking for moral support.

"I call it *kiss up*, Relo said, under his breath.

"No, no. Tomasa's right Relo," said Lu Wang with a chuckle and coming to the waitress's defense, "I suppose steamed rice is a cheap price to pay for keeping our customers happy."

And so every Tuesday, as marked on the calendar, Tomasa packed the food for Relo and Xavier to deliver to the distant restaurants.

"The sit-in eatery was prospering fairly well, so we decided to discontinue the noon runs to the fields and orchards. The restaurant was now open Tuesdays through Saturdays, eleven in the morning until eleven at night. It still maintained its small café atmosphere with the original twelve tables and a long western style bar with twenty stools that we added shortly after we opened. The place was packed just about every night. And as if that was not busy enough for us, the establishment also saw a steady flow of take-out orders," Lu smiled with content.

"As the years went by, I gradually got involved with the community and its activities. I felt that I needed to give back to those that made the business a success. Sunday afternoons I taught an hour long art class, which focused on the art form of *Shan shui* and water coloring. Being an accomplished artist my personal paintings went for a nice price but I always donated the money to charities. It was my way of giving back."

"On Monday evenings and Saturday mornings I taught a beginner's class in *Kung Fu*. On Saturday and Thursday mornings I would also do an additional hour of the martial arts class for the advanced students. A major portion of my advanced class was law enforcement officers from the county sheriff and surrounding police departments."

"I was an honorary sheriff's deputy and would often patrol with another officer on Sunday and Monday nights. My disdain for distributors and drug dealers served as fuel for my deep passion to rid the streets of these people. They were ruining the future of our young kids and wrecking the homes and families of many in the local communities. While on patrol I often requested to be assigned to the unit working the Asian neighborhoods. I always believed that taking care and fixing my own neighborhood should take precedence before reaching across into bordering communities. I always wore the badge with honor and pride. I never flaunted my authority, but instead reached out to help those in times of personal crises and encouraged them to use their talents and lives to help others."

"The drug trafficking problem is not an easy problem to solve, Dexter. Many in the Asian community do not trust the local authorities and feel bound by loyalty to their race. They are tight lipped when it comes to squealing on their own people. Opium and heroin are readily available in the Asian communities, but nabbing the king pin is not an easy task.

Dealings are done behind closed doors, so catching the dealer at the street level is nearly impossible. It always seems that as soon as a dealer is busted another one is out there the following night," Lu Wang tried to point out the seriousness of the ongoing fight against drugs. "I suppose coming from me might not carry much weight, but it's a war that needs to be fought. I would always tell my fellow law enforcement officers, 'The only way to slay the dragon is to cut its head off'. I so much wanted to be the one to slay that beast."

"Lu, what one thing do you consider your greatest contribution to Asian community?" Dexter asked during one of his interviews.

"Well Dexter," he started, "once the business was on its feet and doing fine, I did what I could to better the neighborhood and the surrounding communities. By working with local authorities, schools, and many concerned citizens I helped sponsor, organize, and establish programs that helped kids stay off the streets and develop a wholesome, meaningful image of their own lives. One of the projects that I was instrumental in establishing was the Asian Cultural Arts Center. I've got to admit that when it finally opened to the public, it was one of the proudest moments in my life. The center boasts an auditorium that seats three hundred and space for volunteers who donate their time after school as tutors. It also has four sound proof practice rooms with pianos. Volunteers sign up to give free piano lessons to children from the local area. A museum of art and history of various Asian cultures occupies a separate building. On the second floor of that same building is the center's business offices and two banquet/conference rooms. Twice a month, experts in fields pertaining to social issues, medicine, and other topics of interest are scheduled to present and discuss those issues."

Dexter listened as Lu humbly spoke, "There are many other deeds and accomplishments that I was given credit for. Many I could not have done without the help of others. Teamwork played an important role in my accomplishments. I received several letters of appreciation and commendation from local officials, schools, community organizations, and law enforcement agencies. I also received many honors from various city mayors including the 'Key to the City' to several cities. The Governor presented me with the 'Outstanding Citizen of the Year for the State of California' and the President of the United States awarded me with two separate national awards. One for community service and another for drafting up and launching the national 'Fight Against Drugs' campaign in the Asian community. That was many, many moons ago."

Dexter later wrote, "*For over fifty-five years Lu Wang cooked and served the best Chinese cuisine in the area. And for over fifty-five years his philanthropic generosity helped develop a community that grew and prospered.*"

▫ ▫ ▫

"Talk to me Lu, about what ever happened to Relo and Tomasa," Dexter prompted the man sitting directly across from him.

"About twenty-five years after we opened the restaurant Relo decided that it was time for him to return to his country. Lu Wang begin sharing a little about his long-time friend and business associate.

"He was like a brother to me. He helped me come to America and helped me start an enjoyable and successful business. He was a hard worker and never demanded much of anything in return," reflected Lu Wang, struggling to maintain his composure when he spoke about his dear friend.

"Through the years Relo kept in touch with his siblings in the Philippines. But since making that voyage on the liner that brought both of us to the United States, Relo had not returned to visit his homeland or his family."

"He always talked about going back and purchasing land. His plans always were to return to the Philippines, grow rice, raise livestock, and along with his brothers, live out a quiet life in his native countryside. After twenty five long years of being separated from them, this seemed to be the right time for him to make that dream come true."

"Relo was a frugal man and through the years saved up a substantial amount of money. His savings, in comparison to Filipino standards, made him quite a wealthy man. He was in every sense of the word, returning to the Philippines Islands a very rich person."

"My business partner and friend proved to be a shrewd and very resourceful entrepreneur. He has and will always succeed in anything he puts his heart into. I truly believe that."

"Before he departed, Relo insisted on transferring his part of the business to me. Although I preferred that Relo remain a partner in the business, he went ahead and had the lawyers draw up the proper documents making the change. I even offered to buy out his half of the business but that offer was flatly rejected."

"He played a major role in getting our restaurant up and going. I'll never forget the hard work and generosity that my little friend from the Philippines contributed to our venture and to our life-long friendship. I miss him very much."

As long as the restaurant was operational, Dexter found out, Lu Wang continued (against Relo's wishes) to send monthly checks to his friend, who now resided on one of the over seven thousand islands that make up the Republic of the Philippines.

"Tomasa", Lu Wang continued, "Stayed with me about thirty years after Relo left. Her husband, Xavier, also stayed on. He helped out with the delivery of food to those other restaurants, the dishwashing, and continued to keep the place clean. I never purchased an industrial dishwasher. Throughout the years all the dishes and eating utensils were washed by hand. It really wasn't a matter of finances, it's just that the kitchen was not large enough to accommodate a commercial dishwasher", he added. "You know, Xavier had many medical problems. He suffered from congestive heart failure and in his last few months his breathing was quite labored due to end stage emphysema. After his death Tomasa only worked a few more weeks."

"Dexter", Lu Wang softly interjected, "Rumors circulated in our small community that Tomasa and I had a romantic relationship on the side. It was true. We were romantically involved from the very start. I believe that Xavier was aware but chose, for whatever reason, not to make it an issue."

"According to Tomasa, their marriage had unraveled years ago. They remained together for the sake of convenience. Although Tomasa and Xavier were still married, when I came onto the scene, their relationship had already evolved into platonic love. I was fairly young back then. She was eight years older than me, but that didn't stop us from getting involved. I was truly in love with her, I guess I still am. I would do anything to protect her and give her a happy life," Lu Wang told his interviewer.

Lu Wang let out a long, slow sigh and silently sat there as if he had finally gotten a heavy burden off his chest.

He confided in Dexter that he had no known relatives, so when the time came his estate would be equally split between Tomasa and the Asian Cultural Arts Center.

"When was the last time you two spoke?" Dexter wanted to know.

"I think it was around three weeks ago", said Lu Wang, "And since the restaurant closed she probably has visited about once a month. She doesn't leave the house much. Tomasa is not in very good health. She too has emphysema and requires the use of oxygen twenty-four hours a day. It's the price she's paying for not breaking that terrible habit. She has always been a stubborn creature and continues to smoke, even though the doctors, have repeatedly, spelled out the consequences. She claims that at this stage of her illness, one more cigarette won't make a difference."

"Although I don't agree with her, I guess her point is well taken," Lu added, as an afterthought laced with a trace of sadness.

◙ ◙ ◙

On this, their last interview, Dexter asked the question that was at the top of his long list of questions he had started with thirty weeks ago.

"Lu, with everything that you have been through in your life and with all you have accomplished, is there anything you regret or anything you would do different?"

It didn't take Lu Wang long to respond. Without hesitation, he simply said, "I have had a wonderful life. God has blessed me abundantly and I in-turn, was able to give back to my community. I believe that if given the opportunity, I would not change a thing. All my actions have been to serve mankind, respect nature, and give my all to those I love."

After a few seconds of silence and as if indicating that the interview had come to an end, Lu Wang looked up and made direct eye contact.

"Dexter, I know that this is our last interview, but I would be honored if you would be present for the scheduled event tomorrow evening. I have already made arrangements with security to include you on the authorized list."

The young interviewer was taken by surprise. He had not expected this offer. Graciously and with humility he accepted the dubious honor.

Satisfied with Dexter's acceptance Lu Wang rose to his feet. The officer in the room approached him and put handcuffs on his wrists. As always, Lu Wang stood tall and erect with his head held high and exited the room. With each step, the chain links attached to the ankle shackles scraped the bare concrete floor.

The following night, Monday the twenty-fourth, at exactly 10:00 P.M., Dexter watched as Lu Wang was escorted into the small chamber and placed on an elevated table similar to those used in medical exam rooms. Mr. Wang was secured on the table with leather straps to his wrists, ankles, and waist. An IV was inserted into a vein in his left arm and a lethal dose of combined drugs was administered.

At precisely 10:15 p.m. Lu Wang was pronounced dead.

Epilogue

Over a period of eight weeks, drugs laced with arsenic resulted in the death of several young addicts. This prompted an investigation into the trafficking of drugs within the Asian community. After several months of undercover work, the investigators were led to a surprising and unexpected place of origin . . . Lu Wang's Restaurant.

Traces of heroin, cocaine, and opium were found on some of the stainless steel food containers used to deliver food. It was surmised that he had started the illegal business years ago when he delivered food to workers in the fields. His activities, the prosecution pointed out, gradually became a monopoly which controlled the trafficking of illegal drugs within a 100 mile radius.

Following the verdict *The Valley Ledger* capitalized on Lu Wang's own words, "*Head of Local Drug Ring Decapitated. The Dragon is Slain.*"

The article read:

> *. . . A jury found Lu Wang, a prominent businessman guilty on ten counts levied against him.*
> *On one count for misuse of powers as a public servant to protect and hide his own personal interests—Guilty.*
> *On three counts for the distribution of three different illegal drugs—Guilty.*
> *On six counts for second degree murder—Guilty . . .*

Tomasa was subpoenaed by the prosecution. She hated to do it, but she was under oath to tell the court the locations where the meals were sent every Tuesday night. She was also asked if she had any knowledge that Lu Wang was smuggling and distributing drugs out of the restaurant in the food containers. She answered, "No. Me and my husband only helped deliver the food." After his sentencing, Lu Wang served two years in the general prison population and was later transferred to the death-roll facility where he spent eight months plus five days.

Four months after Lu Wang's execution, Tomasa lost her battle with emphysema. Her computer contained the names of every person involved in the drug ring. She had meticulously recorded every transaction. Prior to the era of computers, she logged every detail in ledgers. According to her entries, the years she worked for Lu Wang proved to be quite lucrative. The restaurant business was a perfect cover up for the trafficking and distribution of illegal drugs. One of her last entries indicated that towards the end, the drugs acquired for distribution were received already tainted with arsenic.

Up until his arrest, not even Lu Wang had the slightest inkling that his food service was being exploited as a front and as a channel for the flow of Tomasa's and Xavier's illegal activities.

Dexter Quinn's documentary, based on Lu Wang, won several national awards and was later made into a full length movie.

A SHORT LOVE STORY

***If** he's a pilot, the man that you love,*
keep in mind, he just might fly off.
If you fret and you wish, and hope he comes home,
be prepared for a surprising outcome.

—*R. Quero*

A Short Love Story

Frances Richards tried to ignore the inappropriate cat calls directed at her as she walked across the parking lot. It was the noon hour and she was on her way to the food court adjacent to the base-exchange (BX) complex at White Lark Air Field, which is located a few miles down the road from Fort Walton Beach in Florida. She was wearing a light summer dress and 3 inch heels that only helped accentuate her nicely shaped calves. She knew she looked sexy and on any other given day would have welcomed the attention she received from the guys on the Air Force base. Frankie, as she preferred to be called, spun around in response to the persistent whistles, only to recognize her two assistants, running to catch up with her.

"Gosh, it's difficult to catch your attention. We're heading off base for lunch, we thought you might want to join us," they offered.

"No thanks, I've been craving the Rueben sandwich they serve at The Deli and I want to get there before they run out. I'll see you in a couple of hours."

She had gotten up late that morning and missed breakfast. The only form of nutrition she had all morning, was a couple of cans of diet drinks and a bran muffin. She was famished and the only thought on here mind this very moment was to get to The Deli and devour their mouthwatering Rueben.

Frances, originally from West Virginia, left the comfort of the classroom environment at a military academy in Denver, Colorado, to conduct seminars on technical writing to military personnel and The Department of Defense civilian employees. Her team was four months into their twenty-four month contract with the government and was scheduled to visit twenty military installations within a period of two years.

She was 25 years old and had always enjoyed traveling. So when the opportunity came up for this assignment, she put a bid in on it and was awarded the contract. Brent and Cheryl, her assistants, also had prior teaching experience at the university level.

It was a beautiful, first day of summer and the fresh breeze coming off the Gulf of Mexico was a welcomed relief after a long morning of enduring a warm stuffy conference room with a faltering air conditioner. It was Friday, June 21st and their next session of the seminar wasn't until 2 P.M. The session was scheduled for two and a half hours and then they would be off for the weekend. Frankie couldn't wait for the time to pass. The previous weekend was a washout but the forecast for this one looked pretty good. She was looking forward to a nice peaceful, sunny weekend on the beach.

Once inside The Deli, she ordered her sandwich and a large glass of iced tea. She eyed and made a beeline to the only available table in the food court, a table for two next to the window. She sat down and slowly started eating her meal while watching the flow of military personnel entering and exiting the BX.

As always, she spent her time watching and mentally picking different characteristics, that she liked, from the men that passed by the window. *That one's too tall. That one is too short. I like that guy's dreamy eyes*; she carefully and secretly built her imaginary idea of the perfect man.

"Excuse me . . . Excuse me ma'am. Is this seat taken? Do you mind if I join you? This is the only open seat," an officer in a flight suit said, interrupting the daydreamer.

Looking up at the five foot eleven inch structure, she apologized, "Oh, I'm sorry. My mind was somewhere else. Sure have a seat," she gestured to the seat in front of her.

"Hi, I'm Rick. Man, I'm starved. I had an early morning flight, got up a little late and missed breakfast."

"Me too," she said laughing. "I mean I missed breakfast too, but I didn't have to fly. I'm Frankie", she introduced herself reaching across the table to shake his hand.

"Nice meeting you, I'm Rick... Rick Barnes," he purposely repeated his name. "Thanks for sharing your table Frankie. Is that your nickname?"

"Yes. My full name is Frances Richards, but everyone calls me Frankie," she explained between bites. "Are you just a Rick?" she asked, admiring his deep rich tan and the fact that he wasn't wearing a wedding band.

"Yep, I'm just Rick. Not Ricky, not Ricardo. I'm just Rick, Rick Barnes," he answered reaching across the table to shake hands again and taking note that she too was not wearing a wedding ring.

"What kind of plane do you fly?" inquired Frankie, admiring his unusual emerald green eyes.

"I fly a surveillance aircraft," Rick informed her. "Do you know much about Air Force airplanes?" he asked, hoping that their conversation would last a little longer than it took to eat a sandwich.

"I'm afraid not. I only know that some are big and some are small. It must be fun and exciting to fly a plane," she told Rick, noting the closely cropped reddish-blond hair after he removed his flight cap.

"Oh, it's a lot of fun and I thoroughly enjoy it. Flying is something I've always wanted to do since I was a kid. And you, what do you do on base?" he asked as he gulped down some iced tea.

"I'm leading a seminar in that big building over there," she answered, pointing at the large complex across the parking lot.

They made small talk, mostly asking questions and trying to learn a little about each other without just coming out and saying, "Okay, just tell me everything I need to know about you."

It was now 1:45 P.M. and the food court had pretty much cleared out. Frankie, glancing at her watch, jumped up realizing her lunch break was over. "I got to go. I have to be back by two," she told him, standing up and moving toward the door.

"Frankie, I'm going to a jazz concert on the beach in Fort Walton tomorrow evening. Would you like to join me?" Rick asked, knowing he had to make a move or risk, possibly, not seeing her again.

"Sure. I was planning on going anyway. I'm staying at the Gulf Beach Condos a block from where the concert is being held. Why don't you come by my place at 5 P.M.? My condo is #107. Maybe we can have a bite to eat before the concert. There's a nice little bistro around the corner from the condos."

"That sounds great. I'll see you tomorrow at five," he called out, as she rushed out the door.

Giving him one last glance and a wide smile, she zinged the strings of his heart with a flirtatious, "See ya tomorrow, Rick."

◻ ◻ ◻

Frankie readied some chilled wine and a tray of cheese, fruit, and crackers. Rick showed up at ten minutes to five with a bottle of the exact wine Frankie was serving.

"Wow, we already have two things in common," Rick stated with confidence. "We both like the same wine and we both enjoy free concerts on the beach."

"I suppose that's not a bad start to a new friendship." Frankie answered, raising her glass to the impromptu toast.

They enjoyed the pre-dinner wine and cheese platter, outside on the patio, overlooking the Gulf of Mexico. A cool breeze coming off the water and the picturesque shoreline added to the pleasant evening on the beach.

At 5:45 P.M. they took the five minute walk along the boardwalk to the bistro. Over a light dinner they both continued getting to know a little more about each other. Rick was in his hometown of Fort Walton Beach. His mother was a published author and had a series of romantic novels, some still in print. She too, lived in Fort Walton Beach.

"Rick, what's your mom's name?"

"Her name is Marsha Willard, but her pen name is Helen Lawrence. Have you ever read any of her books?"

"No, I'm really not into romance books. I'd rather read suspense and autobiographies. But maybe someday I'll read one of your Mom's books."

After dinner they walked back to the beach and worked their way through the crowd to get closer to the stage for the free jazz concert.

Frankie and Rick dated twice a week for a whole month. Every Saturday they attended the free concerts on the beach that showcased the latest tunes in the world of jazz, blues, rock, and country music. Music, laughter, and the hot, humid temperatures filled the summer air during their weekends together.

On Sundays they made it a point to meet for brunch at one of several local restaurants in the coastal city of Fort Walton Beach.

During the week Rick normally flew off to participate in military exercises that are routinely held throughout the summer months. For the most part, his missions were considered sensitive in nature. So Rick was unable to share with her where he went and what he did. If it was a routine exercise he would say he was flying to Nevada, California, or wherever the training was taking place. Otherwise he would just say, "I was on a special training exercise." That was Frankie's cue not to ask questions. Fortunately, Rick was able to have all his weekends off during that one month they were getting to know each other.

At first, Frankie thought it odd that anytime they had to go a distance from the condo Rick would prefer taking the cab, even though she offered to let him drive her car. He eventually told her that his driver's license had been suspended for thirty days. He was embarrassed about the whole situation, but opted to give up his license in lieu of spending time in the city jail.

"It was a couple of days before we met," Rick confided in Frankie. "I had just gotten promoted to the rank of Captain and my buddies threw a promotion party for me and three other guys that were also promoted. It was the first time I had been inebriated and I made the stupid mistake of getting behind the wheel of the car. I was stopped a block from my Mom's house for rolling through a stop sign."

Things seemed to be moving at a fast pace for Frankie and Rick. One thing that bothered her was whether Rick's incident with alcohol was a single incident or a trend. She didn't want to directly address the issue for fear that he might feel like she didn't really trust or believe him. Hopefully, in time, the truth would surface. Up to this point, Rick never had more than two drinks during the course of any given evening they spent together. So maybe this was not an issue at all and there was no need to dwell on it.

The one thing she could not deny, however, were her strong feelings for him that seemed to grow with each passing day. Even Rick had expressed romantic feelings to her and because of his actions, appeared quite genuine and sincere. And she, she confessed to herself, felt comfortable with the thoughts of maybe spending the rest of her life with him.

Frankie was pleasantly surprised, one evening, when she sat down and compared Rick with her mental list of the perfect guy.

Everything I have ever considered as a positive trait in a man, Rick possesses. His features, his interests, and his demeanor are all on the plus side of my list. He's a wonderful cook, has a great sense of humor, and makes me feel like I'm on a continuous cloud-nine ride.

"I think I'm in love," she said out loud, holding the list of positive traits and her daily diary close to her bosom.

▫ ▫ ▫

After a month of dating Rick and spending every Saturday and Sunday together, Frankie suddenly stopped receiving calls from him. At first she thought, *maybe he's on some special mission.* So for four weeks she went around, concerned but not too overly worried about him not calling or dropping by. She never thought about getting his phone number because he was always in contact with her. But now she wished she had a number to call.

Like in every relationship, when one doesn't hear from the other half, she too started to feel like she was being ignored, or maybe just simply being dumped. Surely this wasn't the case. *Why would Rick just suddenly drop me without an explanation?* Frankie wondered. *Did he meet someone else?* she fretted.

Desperate and concerned, she even tried to track him down through the special operations squadron on base. But trying to get information from those secretive organizations was like trying to penetrate the most top clandestine operations of the CIA. No one was divulging any information about any of their flyers, nor the missions their units were involved with.

▫ ▫ ▫

After a month of the silent treatment, Frankie decided to try and contact Rick's Mom. She hated making that call, primarily because she had never met Ms. Willard. But having reached the point of feeling completely rejected, used, and unfairly left in the dark, she needed to find out where she stood.

Marsha Willard's phone number and address were listed in the local phone directory. She reluctantly, called the number and briefly spoke with

Rick's Mom. Ms. Willard sounded a lot older, over the phone, than what Frankie had anticipated. Her voice quivered when she spoke and she kept saying, "I'm sorry, the batteries in my hearing aids are low. I can barely hear you."

She didn't seem to understand or clearly hear what Frankie was saying or talking about. "Would it be all right if I dropped by this evening and spoke with you in person?" Frankie asked.

Ms. Willard agreed, "But only if you come by before it gets dark. Preferably before 6 P.M. I go to bed early."

"I can be there at 5:00 P.M, if that's a good time for you?" Frankie offered.

"Yes, yes . . . that will be fine," she answered, and hung up the phone.

The Marsha Willard that answered the door of the quaint beach cottage was an eighty-two year old with long hair colored dark black. She had large round eyes, wore a beret, and resembled an eccentric looking character out of the 1950's. She walked slightly stooped, her back afflicted with scoliosis.

"Welcome young lady. Please come in." Ms. Willard led her through a dimly lit foyer into a musty smelling front room that contained mounds of books everywhere. They were crammed into book cases, stacked on tables, and were the main ingredient for the pillars of books that appeared to grow up and out of the wooden floors. The books created a maze, challenging them as they maneuvered their way to the sitting room.

"I understand that you're a writer", Frankie mentioned, trying to strike up a conversation.

"Yes, yes dear, I've written several books, mostly romance and mystery novels. I've slowed down in my writing. I guess I probably write a story about every two years. Mostly, I just enjoy reading, as you can see from my collection. Did you bring the book you wanted me to sign?"

"Oh, I'm sorry," Frankie apologized, "But I'm not here for an autograph. I've never even read any of your novels. I'm Frankie. Frances Richards. Remember I spoke with you earlier on the telephone. I'm here because I'm dating your son and I haven't seen him in over a month."

"I think I'm a little confused. I don't know what you're talking about," Ms. Willard said with a puzzled look.

"Ms. Willard . . . You are Marsha Willard whose pen name is Helen Lawrence? Are you not?"

"Yes. Yes, that's me. But please call me Marsha. Now, what is it you want from me?"

"Marsha, as I mentioned I've been dating your son Rick. I guess he never mentioned me to you."

"My dear, what in the world are you talking about?" the aged writer asked.

Taking into account that Marsha Willard was probably suffering from dementia, Frankie again, slowly and louder addressed her, "Marsha, I am Frankie and am dating your son Rick. I am concerned about his whereabouts."

"Yes, yes my dear. But please don't yell. I have fresh batteries in my hearing aids. Is this some kind of a prank? What do you mean you are dating my son Rick?"

Realizing Rick had not even mentioned her to his mom, Frankie decided to explain to Ms. Willard the reason for paying her a visit.

"You see Ms. Willard, I met Rick on June 21st and we spent every Saturday and Sunday of the following four weeks together," Frankie told her, completely filling his Mom in on her relationship that had developed between her and Rick.

After patiently listening to Frankie's side of the story, Marsha stood up and asked Frankie to follow her to a smaller room that appeared to be an art studio. There were paintings covering every square inch of the walls. Many were leaning against anything that could prop them up.

"Frankie, see if you can find a painting of Rick for me."

Frankie searched the walls crowded with wonderful paintings. They were all signed by Marsha Willard.

"My God, you certainly are a wonderful artist," she said as she continued to search through stacks of paintings. "Here he is," she announced as she pulled a 24" x 48" portrait out of a group of oil paintings. "Wow, you painted him too," she smiled admiring the portrait of her boyfriend and recognizing Ms. Willard's signature on the canvas.

"Yes, yes my dear, that's the one. Are you sure you've never read any of my books?" Marsha asked, raising her penciled eyebrows and peering at her through her thick, red rimmed glasses.

"That's right Marsha. I'm sorry but your genre does not particularly fall into my field of interest."

The loud chimes from an antique grandfather clock, in the hallway, announced the half hour.

"Sweetie, please join me for some hot tea. It's time for my medication and I take it with hot tea," Marsha said, as she exited the art studio and shuffled her way to the kitchen. Frankie followed, admiring the paintings on the walls. Marsha had a story for each and every painting. It took them a several minutes to get to the kitchen.

"I painted most of my family members, many of my friends, and did a lot of beach scenes. A lot of the paintings on the walls were used as illustrations in my novels. "As a matter of fact," Marsha let it be known, "I painted all the illustrations for my books."

Passing through the living room, Marsha grabbed a book from a tall stack of novels and blew the dust off. Once in the kitchen, Marsha poured two cups of hot tea as she continued to explain each painting and their significance. When they sat down at the kitchen table, Marsha slid the thin book across the table toward Frankie. "I would like you to have this novel. It's a love story and probably the shortest novel I've ever written," she told her lovely guest.

"Frankie, my dear, I painted that portrait of Rick in his flight suit and I used that same oil painting as the illustration for my novel."

"How nice of you to write a story about your own son," Frankie interjected.

"Yes, yes my dear, but there's more you should know about our Rick . . . much more." Marsha Willard alias Helen Lawrence, continued, "In my novel, Rick went AWOL, that means absent without leave, you know; He wanted to spend time with his girlfriend. Upon returning to his unit at the air base, he was given the choice of going on a dangerous secret mission or spending time in the *brig* for going AWOL. He chose to fly the mission. During that mission, shortly after he penetrated enemy airspace, his plane was shot down. I ended the story with Rick Barnes missing in action."

Now it was Frankie's turn to be perplexed. "What are you talking about? I don't under . . . ." She started expressing her confusion, before being interrupted.

"Sweetie, in my novel Rick went AWOL on June 21st for thirty days. The very same day you said you first met Rick and the exact number of days you said you dated him. The portrait I painted of Rick Barnes was my concept for the main character in this novel," she explained, tapping the book with her long, bony, index finger. "I created him in my mind, painted him on canvas, made up a name, and wrote about him in this short love story nearly sixty years ago. I suppose one might call me his mother. I've never thought of it like that. Anyway, please read the novel. And if my Rick Barnes is 'your Rick Barnes' and if 'your story' is not a silly prank on this old woman, then I suspect you will never see him again. You see, Rick Barnes is still missing in action . . . just like in my novel."

Note to the Reader

I hope you enjoyed at least one, two, or three (if not more) of the stories in this book. They were intended as fun and easy reading. If anything, I hope they at least got your creative juices flowing and you too will take the time to put your thoughts, imagination, or hidden writing skills on paper.

Now, I know that not every ending of every story will please everyone. So this is your chance . . . . Feel free to write in the margins of these pages (that is, if this book belongs to you) and rewrite the ending to your satisfaction.

Acknowledgements

I know that behind everyone that has a story or book to share, there is at least one person who had an influence in his or her writings. In my case there are several. So I want to take the opportunity to thank the following individuals for helping to make this book a reality. For always being there, thanks for your thoughts, prayers, and unconditional love: Gerald Ferguson, Yolanda Montgomery, Rita Quero, Victoria Escoto, Virginia Flores, Frances Steen, and Lawrence Quero.

Thanks also to Mary Gettle, for the inspiration and support you have given me. Our late night, long distant phone calls, over the past forty-plus years, have been a great source of encouragement.

Many thanks to my relatives and friends, who in one way or another, have also been an inspiration. For those of you, who have read some of my stories, thanks for the inputs and suggestions.

And I mustn't forget Terry I. Miles . . . Thanks for meeting me at the local coffee shop, sharing your expertise, and taking the time to read my rough manuscript. Your smile is always a welcome sight.

For editing the majority of these stories, Celine Rose Mariotti, you have taught me the importance of breaking-up and rewriting several of my long narratives. Thank you for all your hard work, guidance, and recommendations. Bear with me; I'm a work in progress.

A special shout out to all the wonderful folks I served with in the military and to those who I presently work with in the medical field. Y'all have been a wonderful source for ideas and have certainly made it, for me, two interesting and rewarding careers.

About the Author

RUBEN QUERO shares his passion for writing with the debut of his first book, ***TEN TWISTS***. With encouragement from family, friends, and co-workers, he took several of his writings and compiled them into this book of short stories. He served twenty and a half years in the United States Air Force and incorporates the experiences and knowledge gained from his travels into many of his stories. Following retirement from the military Ruben attended Respiratory Therapy School and has worked as a respiratory care practitioner in Southern Mississippi and Louisiana. His is presently employed as a staff respiratory therapist at a major medical center in New Orleans, LA.

With now over twenty years in the medical field, he allows the training, the experiences, the situations, and the myriad of personalities encountered, to serve as fodder for many of his stories.

Originally from Southern California, Ruben graduated from Ventura High School and Ventura College. He also graduated from the Community College of the Air Force, the Mississippi Gulf Coast Community College, and the University of Southern Mississippi.

His hobbies include gardening, painting, writing, and traveling. He is a member of the Gulf Coast Writers Association and has had short stories published in specialty magazines.

He resides in Diamondhead, MS, a community located along the beautiful Mississippi Gulf Coast.

For updates on Ruben Quero's writings and to view some of his paintings visit www.worksbyruben.com.